REQUIEM FOR A SOLDIER

REQUIEM
FOR A SOLDIER

Oleg Pavlov

Translated by
Anna Gunin

LOS ANGELES · HIGH WYCOMBE

First published in English translation in 2015 by And Other Stories
Los Angeles – High Wycombe
www.andotherstories.org

Copyright © Oleg Pavlov, 2002

Published by arrangement with ELKOST Intl. Literary Agency

English language translation copyright © Anna Gunin, 2015

ISBN: 9781908276582
eBook ISBN: 9781908276599

Editors: Sophie Lewis & Louisa-Claire Dunnigan; proofreader: Louise
Scothern; typesetter: Tetragon, London; typeface: Swift Neue & Verlag;
cover design: Hannah Naughton; cover image: courtesy of the Library
of Congress Prints and Photographs Division, Washington, DC.

Printed and bound in Great Britain
by TJ International Ltd, Padstow, Cornwall

A catalogue record for this book is available from the British Library.

This book was supported using public funding by Arts Council England
and with the support of the Institute for Literary Translation (Russia).

Supported using public funding by

ARTS COUNCIL
ENGLAND

ИНСТИТУТ ПЕРЕВОДА

AD VERBUM

MIX
Paper from
responsible sources
FSC® C013056

CONTENTS

Rejoice, O young man, in thy youth

Ecclesiastes

GENESIS

They were still selling watermelons in the wind and the cold, while Karaganda sailed on the steppe winds deeper and deeper into the approaching winter. Every morning the clouds would timidly disperse, having come out of hiding during the night to hang among the crushed crumbs of scattered stars. November's widescreen monochrome sky was laid bare. Out of the stone slab of day came forth the cold, which sulkily prowled the streets, the avenues, the squares – spaces where the surging winds swayed the raft-like columns of russet trees. The prison guard regiment switched over to winter time as it had always done: on the scheduled day when the order was given. Decked out in greatcoats, the camp's guards and sentries were adapting to their warmer underclothes. The only ones stubbornly looking forward to the start of each new day were the men confined for treatment in the regimental infirmary.

There was seldom a peep louder than a mouse from the occupants of the infirmary. Those souls kept quiet, dosed up on their medicines. The mice, though, made quite a din: those voracious little grey wretches were everywhere. As the weather cooled, they had migrated from the garden, where the harvest had already been gathered, to the cellar and wall cavities in the shack-like infirmary – a building that proved fateful even for them. The mice entertained the prisoners in the infirmary, sometimes even comforting them, striking up hearty friendships when it took their fancy and with anyone they pleased if beckoned with a mere crust of bread. This was where they came into the world, beneath the floorboards and between the walls, but they were rarely seen as corpses, save by the one man who hunted them down with a passion, day in, day out: the head of the infirmary, who had a funny-sounding surname and hated with a vengeance all forms of life that gave out even the tiniest autonomous squeak.

The infirmary mice chomped their way through so many different drugs that you'd think they were suffering from every ailment at once and even laying in stores prophylactically. In the space of a year they had already devoured several sacks of Novalgin alone. The tablets had first emboldened the mice to the point of stupor, then made them as clever as geniuses, but they hadn't been killed – well, all medicines are tested on mice, after all, before getting the green light for industrial production. And the man who went by the name of Institutov knew it all too well. Those mice were the only ones who could stand up to the military medic, and they roamed freely.

The head of the infirmary was no servile old trooper, neither in temperament nor in spirit. At some point he had been enlisted to work as a dental technician, having been to vocational college, which distinguished him considerably from everybody else, and at moments when he felt the need to remind people who they were dealing with, he would declare imposingly: 'Well, being a man with a college education, I . . . '

As with all the civilian staff, in the interests of uniformity and equality they bestowed upon him the rank of junior officer. But Institutov did not have to go chasing ignominiously after promotion. When the previous head had drunk himself irrevocably into oblivion, they appointed the teetotal toothpuller in his place: a man of medium height with a neatly clipped moustache, a dull complexion and arms that were short and unremarkable but had amassed muscle with the help of an almost daily regimen of weight training. Institutov fastidiously and at times even fearfully abhorred anything plain and simple, so his workout with kettle bells, for example, he called his 'kettle-bell sport', and whenever he gave an ordinary jab, it became an 'outpatient procedure'. Although the toothpuller cut rather a hefty figure, he tried to accentuate his elegance and beauty – yet the only feature to exude allure or power was his innately dark, teetotal eyes that glinted like anthracite. Sometimes they would narrow suddenly with malice and resentment like two little devils, while at other times a pair of sleek, rotund, magnificent demons would surface imperially from their depths, meaning the head of the infirmary was feeling content.

Institutov made a habit of judging people: whenever he felt irked, he would liken their personalities to characters from literary works, and not even necessarily to bad characters. No person held the slightest novelty for him. He would remark, with a note of exasperation, 'You're hardly the first of your ilk.' That's not to say he had read widely or seen much of life. But he had an inkling of things, having picked up a smattering of this and that, and at the sight of living people he would grimace like an erudite man faced with some phoniness.

The head of the infirmary abhorred alcohol; it seemed as though sober living was one of his most firmly held principles, perhaps even an ethical ideal. The reality was he suffered from a stomach ulcer, but he kept hush, ashamed that his body could host so common and primitive an ailment. Alcohol was always to hand in the infirmary, so it was odd to see spirits freely available and the head of the infirmary strutting about like some scrupulous insect, while across the street was a hostel for prison staff without a drop of drink in sight where everyone would always be horribly drunk and you'd hear a wail of singing, raucous hollering, children bawling, and a fanfare of dishes clattering and smashing.

For Institutov, service in the infirmary was all one long jittery race. He never found the time to treat people. Almost the entire day was taken up with important and shadowy matters that may have borne a semblance to disease, but only because they smacked of fatal outcomes. He was oblivious to the idea that in such cases people could be driven by diligence, or profit, or fear – his only desire was to be rid of the troubling business just as soon as he could. On each occasion it was merely due to his squeamishness that he carried out his work in the finest possible manner, contriving throughout to sparkle with squeaky cleanliness and thus validate one of the epithets applied to his profession: 'men in white coats'. Institutov had the odious feeling that they were using him for their own ends as a clean-up person in cases where they were afraid of getting their own hands dirty, but all he could do was revolt inwardly in silence or suffer senselessly, despising those above him. Indeed, it seemed typical of him to carry something out despite the torment, and be in torment while he carried it out.

He had for a long time been too idle to treat people's teeth, or perhaps he just couldn't abide unclean and malodorous mouths, preferring instead to whip the teeth out – especially for the lower ranks. In his daily work as a dentist, one moment inflicting pain, the next eliminating it, he personally felt little – he just got on with the job. And he would tell his patients, 'Well, what can we do? My friend, be brave – I'm the dentist, not the pain.' His patients would approach him in dread of perhaps the most daunting pain known to man. They would tremble before him, throw themselves at his feet – though it was simply the toothache filling them with fear. The toothpuller from time to time would sense the delicious power he held over people, but unable to find anything else to lust after, he kept on passionately obliterating those mice.

It was not from existential boredom that Institutov succumbed to the temptation to strew poison and set up a blunt little mouse guillotine – and when he stamped some of the wretches out, he felt no heartache. In the whole wide world he loved only himself, and then not even with that blind familial love directed towards one's own blood, but lustfully, lasciviously, the way one person's flesh hungers incessantly for the flesh of someone still lovelier. But his entire paradise on earth was being wrecked on a daily basis by the mice, who could only be moved to act through fright. He was especially aghast and aggrieved whenever he found right there in his pockets fresh mouse droppings, which were not only white in colour but tablet-shaped. Those ever-present grey creatures were alone to blame for everything. Sometimes Institutov would mumble, 'They're trying to kill me,' and he'd scowl with a haunted air, utterly miserable and pitiful. At other times he would denounce them out loud: 'They don't want to pull their weight in society!' And the fact he was powerless to tackle those pilfering rascals, who were forever stealing brazenly from the infirmary, was well and truly driving him insane. Those grey little brutes were the cause of his anguish, much like the anguish experienced by people with toothache who fancy their entire life is convulsing piteously, racked by a great tapeworm of pain. Institutov could understand the mice when they squeaked. He knew almost all of them by sight and was quite sure that the mouse scurrying under the cabinet in his office was the very same one he'd seen last week in the treatment room or some such place. He remembered precisely which mouse had been stealing, all the outrages it had got up to and the overall harm it posed. He saw mice as a breeding ground for every contagious disease, from cholera to the plague, claiming for some reason that mice lived and fed only on refuse, despite the fact that they lived and ate alongside him, sometimes even right next to him in his office, feeding from his own forgotten biscuit left lying on the table. Yet the chief crime of these wretches apparently lay in the fact that, as Institutov would have it, they were plotting to kill him. From time to time he had feverish visions of them scaling his body, gnawing through his throat or veins and then crawling right into his mouth. Hence the head of the infirmary was, in some deeper sense, not so much possessed of a murderous passion to eradicate their entire genus as tirelessly battling to save his own life.

Yet the various chemical poisons that tasted of saltpetre seldom worked on them; it was as if the rodents had long ago discovered an antidote among the drugs they fed on in the infirmary. At his own expense, Institutov had purchased a large batch of mousetraps, and ever since he'd been filling them up with delicious-smelling bait bought with his own hard-earned cash. Every other mouse, benefitting from experience, patiently ate around the traps, dining as Institutov's guest, and then made haste each month to bring fresh additions into the world. So it was impossible to wipe them out unless you could destroy them all at once – say, by setting fire to the infirmary. Towards nightfall, as the head of the infirmary left the scene of his battle for survival, the mice would emerge, parading in columns. The lights were not yet out, but everyone was already tucked up in bed ready for sleep. Then they would sweep forth in ranks across the vast flat expanse of linoleum, like little soldiers in overcoats in their grey pelts. Chances were only the most battle-hardened took part in these parades – their motions were resolute and harmonised. After gliding round in a circle, the mouse militia would vanish, to general laughter. Then the lights went out and everyone fell asleep in blissful silence, while the mice did battle somewhere else, valiantly surviving to see another morning.

The toms and she-cats that Institutov from time to time brought in to the infirmary for mouse-catching did not stay put for long; given a day or two, they would ingloriously scarper, shinning up the apple trees in the garden and then dropping out of them like wailing comets onto their tarmac home turf. The first of the felines to flee had acquired the name of Barsik, and ever since, this name somehow attached itself to all the other cats. People would stroke a Barsik; they would give it some milk. But the animals nonetheless wanted their freedom. The head of the infirmary, it should be mentioned, detested pretty much all animals, as if in his eyes they were somehow all descended from those abominable mice. He would quite gladly have strangled and hanged the cats, who also fed on the scraps and were forever brazenly pilfering things from people, if it weren't for his need of them – and so he caught them in the refuse and smuggled them into the infirmary in the bottom of his briefcase, all wrapped up fastidiously in plastic bags. After their suffocating ordeal in the briefcase, no force on earth could keep the Barsiks within the walls of the infirmary, where all but one of the wards usually stood empty.

Come what may, the head of the infirmary had to cling on to his patients. Anyone who recovered would be fed until his cheeks grew as plump and flush as a bashful maiden's, and they were condemned to interminable treatment. Someone needed to scrub the place to that squeaky cleanliness which Institutov so admired; someone had to listen to his sermons and to toil away for their own good – and it wouldn't be the ward attendants, who'd become insolent from idleness and who filled him with fear. So it was the dexterous and docile lads who were on his books for months as contagious patients and whose illnesses had gradually mutated into chronic disease. In their own units they had been guarding convicts, some as guards, others as sentries, but from the moment they found themselves in the infirmary they were confined indoors for upwards of a month. They had been born in a variety of places and circumstances, but all in the same period. So they had more or less all turned eighteen when the call-up came. At first, in the mass of their own kind, all camouflaged in grassy, earthy colours, they would run, then crawl, then march imposingly in the same direction, but their sense of self faded as they all merged into one, and they were blithely unaware of what lay ahead. It wasn't a unit or a herd or a throng – no, it was the people itself, with its own mission, yet also with a personality of its own. Childishly trusting – and already more or less cowed. Incredibly resilient – and yet moaning and groaning at the slightest complaint. Hale and hearty – and yet bone idle. It was as if they had all entered this world in their parents' footsteps only to cross into manhood and manage before dying to leave in their wake some similarly trusting, resilient, moaning, hearty, idle child. Many of those whom fate had escorted to the infirmary would sneeringly tell the same dull old story about their close shave with death. The only ones to keep quiet were those hiding in the corner hoping to end it all. And among them all there'd be some true hero who'd been burnt in the arms depot and fought back the flames to prevent an explosion after he'd torched the place himself while trying to make an electric kettle element out of a high-voltage knife switch.

Life in an infirmary bed may have been a good deal more nourishing than in the army barracks, to say nothing of the prison camp, but the mere words 'sick list' and 'infirmary contingent' were enough to send the brains of yesterday's guards and sentries into a crazy whir until they burned with a longing for freedom. All the quirks of life here suddenly turned into a reflection of the stinking prison and the lousy camp, with their regimes, inmates and miserable black void. The sensation of walking in front of yourself down the straight, narrow corridor as if being led under guard took some getting used to. The smug, imperious glances of those who'd breezed in from the outside bruisingly knocked the composure from your shoulders.

The dressing gown issued in the infirmary somehow had a demeaning effect.

The officers' ward, which had always been filled with nothing but mice and a desolate emptiness, one day became charged with a particularly oppressive silence. With the arrival of a young lieutenant at the infirmary, it had become gloomy for no clear rhyme or reason. On the day of his admission, the new patient was escorted by two officers who didn't look like medical staff and, what's more, with their faces clad in bronze tans they were clearly not locals. The entire party was still free of overcoats. They must have been serving on the edge of the steppes, where come spring or autumn the sun blazed like in the desert, and where boredom and the blues could drive men out of their minds. From that faraway place this lieutenant had been brought to Karaganda under the escort of officers – and all just to put him in an ordinary infirmary. His escorts stood like heathen idols waiting to receive the officer's dusty, faded uniform, which had slipped off stocking-like as though it were a cast skin. With the uniform in their arms, they briskly vanished, carrying out the wishes of some unseen person. The lieutenant whose clothing had been taken – stripping him perhaps of his uniform, perhaps of his freedom – was issued a gown from the infirmary's stores, one so roomy yet so tattered that the officer looked like a mendicant even in the lonely, fully enclosed garden, where they spotted him coming out for a smoke. They also saw him each morning in the utility room, where he washed and took his time carefully shaving.

Institutov ran the infirmary as though it were his home, and you couldn't take a step without his house-proud chidings and proddings. There can't have been a woman alive who could have stomached that rancorous old-maidish behaviour, which was why Institutov, no matter how he bent over backwards to please the ladies, was still knocking about as a barren old bachelor. With the punctiliousness of a eunuch, the head of the infirmary not only tried to knock everyone and everything into shape, but would also offer a running commentary of tedious speeches. Whatever living beings or even inanimate objects turned up in the infirmary, Institutov would immediately form his own opinion of them, and they were all expected to indulge his needs, not only by following his rules but also by listening to his lectures. When the lieutenant made his appearance, though, Institutov kept a wary silence and carefully avoided contact with this new person, as if the strange young man had been placed in the infirmary for purposes other than treatment. No doubt the real reason for keeping him in the infirmary was indeed known to him, and that was why he avoided the officers' ward, merely muttering once or twice as he glanced in its direction, 'Fancies himself a Raskolnikov, eh . . . '

When Institutov decided to put the new arrival into some kind of quarantine, his eyes happened to alight on one of his soldier charges, who was already hard at work painting, towering above him near the ceiling all alone on the trestle.

The head of the infirmary became engrossed for a moment in an icy tingle of conscience that was pricking him, but with a somewhat asinine pomposity he called out, 'Kholmogorov! Come, my friend, get down from the heavens . . . ' The soldier dropped what he was doing and clumsily descended from the trestle's height – half-naked and splodged from head to toe in whitewash, he looked like some gypsum figure adorning a park. Glancing at the foolish statue with his drooping arms, Institutov frowned and said, 'Well, my friend, I have a new job for you: to serve breakfast, lunch and supper in the officers' ward and, when our new patient has finished, you can take away the dirty dishes.'

THE ETERNAL TOOTH

It had been a month since another boss had thrust this demobilised dead soul upon Institutov's infirmary: warrant officer Abdullayev, head of the firing range, who went by the nickname of Abdulka. The deaf and useless old soldier held sway out in the desolate steppe, a hundred kilometres from Karaganda. Abdullayev had previously served in one of the prison guard companies, but during some field exercises held on the anniversary of the October Revolution, he'd been maimed. Two fateful events had occurred on that day in the make-believe zone of hostile fire. First, he had stumbled and fallen, and second, right at the spot where he fell, as if on cue, a thunderbolt had exploded mimicking a blast as a hundred-odd men in khaki were acting out the shift from defence to offence.

From the watchtower somebody continued to gaze down on the soldierly swarm of little men in khaki, and the only annoyance – a brief one, no doubt – came when one ant-like man let out a scream, began bleeding profusely, and lay there unable to fathom why this had happened to him. Abdullayev was left facing the cruel fate of an invalid consigned to the scrap heap.

It was his sheep that saved him – his own humble yet lovingly tended livestock. On someone's suggestion, Abdullayev had offered a lamb to each man on the medical commission and in the unit who had any sway over his fate. And each of them duly reasoned that a man who was deaf, in all senses of the word, could in fact be endowed with hearing. Mindful that the shell-shock victim no longer complained of hearing loss, one by one the recipients of the lambs declared Abdulla Ibrahimovich Abdullayev fit for service, that is to say, as right as rain. The last man to stick his neck out and allow the deaf man to stay in service offered him a livelihood in the farthest-flung place of all: the training ground, quiet as a graveyard, a sandy, rocky site in the steppe, all bashed up with bullets and blasts. Thus the wild and barren spot where he'd been robbed of his hearing – robbed of half his life, as it had seemed – had turned the deaf little man in khaki into an army boss.

To keep in their good books, once a year the shell-shocked man would visit his benefactors bearing something delicious to eat.

Abdulka always had one private reporting to him, in line with his entitlement. He must have been the only commander in the regiment with just one man in his charge. For the bulk of the year, during the weeks and sometimes months when the firing ceased, the deaf man lived with his missus in a small rural settlement, only visiting the distant training ground for the sake of propriety, while in summer and winter his single soldier would dwell in the wild, arid steppe, keeping watch over the wind. Fatherly old Abdulka doted on all his little soldiers and he'd reminisce about them as though they were sons, each becoming his one and only when the time came for them to part. These privates of his were odd creatures – as good as masters of all that Abdullayev personally presided over for barely a month in the year. They would arrive at his training ground all much the same – strangers, gazing about the steppes like doomed men. When they left a few years later, each unfailingly superseding the last in this post in the plains, they were still largely alike – beloved sons, eyes brimming with the enlightenment of sages, some already going grey at the tender age of twenty. That autumn Abdullayev had just lost the latest to be demobbed. The soldier should have left for home long ago. But fatherly old Abdulka couldn't let him go just like that: he decided to bestow on him an eternal steel tooth.

The explosion, his own bloodcurdling scream, the sight of blood running from his ears – everything terrible that occurred at the firing ground that day had shaken and shocked Abdulka so deeply that, ever since, all manner of things would conjure in him a feeling of eternity. Abdullayev had already had some metal teeth fitted, even a gold one, but he'd never before reflected on the fact that they would remain after he was gone; that, say, in a thousand years' time some-one might find them in his grave. This touching and timid desire to contain something eternal had moved Abdulka to get his healthy teeth replaced with ones of steel, and from then on his life's pride and joy were those stainless chinks of eternity, gleaming and glinting in the sun whenever the shell-shocked man lost his temper or grinned. To give a steel tooth to his latest son was like sharing this triumph of human life between the two of them. 'What kind of man are you, without a tooth? Nothing to shout about, eh, just ashes and dust. You're like the sand – one puff of wind and you'll come to grief!' Abdulka spoke loudly; like all deaf men, he couldn't hear what he was saying, and his voice boomed as though from a loudspeaker.

The soldier didn't protest, believing that the shell-shocked man meant him nothing but good. Abdulka paid Institutov a visit, bearing a lamb carcass wrapped up like a log in hessian – he was offering this generous gift of his own accord and only out of naïvety. Institutov would have softened at the sight of a mere leg of lamb, but Abdulka was already pining so badly for his cherished soldier that no powers of reason or forces of any description could make him diminish his sacrifice.

Just behind fatherly Abdulka, decked out in dress uniform and looking almost guilty, stood that soldier. He was like an overgrown child lost in a fog of bewilderment ever since emerging into the world. He had with him his soldier's identity papers, a cash payment of forty-five roubles that he'd just been issued in the regiment's accounting department, and a document entitling Private Aleksei Mikhailovich Kholmogorov to a second-class ticket to anywhere in the whole vast country.

Quick on the uptake, the pragmatic head of the infirmary did not heap praise upon the generous soul of Abdulla Ibrahimovich; rather he vowed to fix the soldier up with the finest steel tooth, placed prominently and bonded to him until death. Abdulka readily believed not so much this man's words as the laws of human life, which he surrendered to like a worker ant, and which, as a human, he could infringe only on pain of instant punishment tantamount to death. And by those laws, no man on earth – no fellow worker ant – could cheat Abdulka once he'd accepted advance payment, because the man wouldn't be able to live with himself afterwards. This was all the assurance Abdulka had wanted when preparing the lamb for Institutov. But upon hearing the word 'death', Abdulka was moved, and suddenly his eyes welled up with tears as if he were at a funeral. The shell-shocked commander followed conversations by reading people's lips, yet people would be taken aback – unless they'd forgotten he was deaf – by the unexpected emotion in his responses to seemingly mundane utterances.

The moment fatherly old Abdulka started weeping, Kholmogorov almost burst into tears himself, feeling somehow orphaned. 'Abdulla Ibrahimovich, I'll get along fine without the tooth, come on, let's be on our way!' Alyosha said. Having already taken payment for his task, the head of the infirmary winced horribly. But the deaf man heard nothing and the soldier, who for some reason felt a pang of conscience, stayed put. Institutov said a long goodbye to the commander of the firing ground, then stole a few glances at the youngster, whose asinine appearance was already riling him. Worried that once Abdulka had gone he could well enough drop in unannounced, Institutov set straight to work and extracted the tooth destined for replacement with a steel one, but after biding his time for a couple of days, he forgot about his debt. At first he insisted that you couldn't produce a tooth to last for centuries in the space of just a few days. Breathing a sigh of relief, Alyosha believed the head of the infirmary. Trust always came more naturally to him than mistrust. He would only stop believing a man once he'd been well and truly duped; before the realisation set in, though, the man would have time to bamboozle him several times over.

Kholmogorov reassured himself: 'It's all right, I'll give it another week and then I'll catch the train and go home.' To make the time pass more quickly, he agreed to do the tasks they set him in the infirmary. But here too it turned out he was helping them not of his own free will; rather, he was paying off Institutov personally for the long-awaited eternal tooth. Kholmogorov could pack up and leave whenever he liked. He had all the documents required, and he'd long ago been taken off the roll. Institutov, though, was ready to tolerate his presence in the infirmary – indeed, to benefit from it. He dared not kick him out for fear Abdulka would catch wind of it. And lately he seemed to have dropped his 'I'll give him the tooth when I feel like it'; instead, he was setting him tasks as his debtor: 'He'll get the tooth when he's earned it.' Indeed, he spelled it right out: 'You, my friend, as it happens, are free to leave.' But as if to spite him, Kholmogorov hung on and waited patiently for what he had been promised.

Alyosha might not have known that great law of life so revered by Abdulka, but he trusted him. And so he had to believe the head of the infirmary, in whom Abdulla Ibrahimovich had placed his trust. Thus the slippery, meaningless promise of tomorrow – that desperate promise made by a restless, cornered little man – suddenly grew into a momentous human truth. Meanwhile, everyone he ran into would ask him how he'd lost his tooth and Alyosha would gladly launch into conversation: 'They've pulled it out to make room for a new one. Was going to be the first to go home, couldn't believe my luck. But I stayed on to mend my teeth and now it's looking like I'll be last to leave. Ah, but it'll save me hassle in the long run. A steel tooth will last me a lifetime.' They tried to shoot down this certainty of his: 'But what if it rusts?' And as they all laughed at him, he too smiled, but with a squirming, faraway smile so disfiguring his face that their sniggers of disgust began to die down and resemble coughs before fading out. Alyosha twitched like a frog wired to the mains; he was happy at the thought they were all listening to him. 'I don't think it'll rust or wear down – life's too short for that. Well it's not like I'm going to live to two hundred! Nobody on Earth can do that yet!'

From time to time he felt sad, of course, sometimes he even ached inside, but an intense wonder for life would burst through the sadness and aching like grass striving towards light. As Alyosha entered adulthood this wonder took such hold over him that to onlookers he'd appear rather dopey and idle, and a holler would usually catch him off guard. Then he'd wake up and knuckle down to work. But if you spurred him on, his innate clumsiness would spoil his work and heighten the problem and he'd begin to wreck things more than fix them.

Alyosha Kholmogorov's soul was like thick porridge – rather than spattering about, all it did was retreat into itself, its warmth gravitating towards stillness. When his soul became suffused with heat, it just puffed up impetuously like a toad's bulging throat. And it always needed time – it was slow to flare up and slow to cool off. Alyosha was loath to relinquish any spot he'd been occupying for even an hour. And whenever his life took a new turn, he would clam up and start living in vibrant memories of the comfortable past. Reticence would overpower him at first – but only until the anxiety passed, the unknown had grown familiar and his life become hum-drum again.

With the trepidation of a man partaking of a divine mystery, Alyosha considered himself graced with luck and worried that this good fortune could vanish just as capriciously as it had been bestowed. But what he counted as lucky was miraculous only to him, for he always got the dregs. He had a compelling sensation that he was different from other people, as if a gift had been conferred on him, and, noticing the shortcomings of those around him, he somehow managed to feel sorry for them, unable to see that he'd have been better off pitying himself. At first glance he looked a sullen, furtive creature, backward and deficient, remarkable only for his clumsiness. When the new conscripts were delivered to the drill ground, this was all that the recruiters saw in him. Each one waved him aside: 'Ha, you can send that knuckle-head off to Abdulka. We've no need for his talents. He'd be one mouth too many for us!' And so they sent him off in a scabby old ambulance without fellow passengers on a one-way journey. Alyosha parted from the regiment, pondering his incredible fortune at being sent somewhere so special and deserted, and what blind faith they had shown in him – or was it recognition? – while the rest of the men, poor souls, were essentially being sent into exile.

Everyone knew and remembered the road to the firing ground. In summer it was a rocky, sun-baked rutted track, and in winter a narrow channel which a tractor had hewn from the marble of the snow banks. It was fifteen kilometres to the nearest inhabited village. Abdulka used to ride out from there on his motorbike.

When they held range practice, for three days on end the companies would arrive one after another at the ground. They unfurled into human chains, dug trenches, did a bit of shooting; afterwards the firing ground would empty and grow still. All its desolate lands stretched beyond the compass of the eye. Such a sweeping expanse could not be enclosed, and so its boundaries were marked by lone posts, spaced within eyeshot of one another. They looked like giant death cap mushrooms, sheltering from heat or rain the sentry guards who were posted there briefly while a profusion of bullets that had missed their targets flew randomly across the steppe and the occasional civilian straying from their path would wander onto the firing ground, dazed by the thunderous roar of guns.

Kholmogorov arrived at the training ground as it fell dark. The tender twilight gloom obscured all that he was so eager to see. The wind was blowing from the dark with an almighty chill and droning in his ears like the whoosh of a seashell. The ambulance headlights melted the dusky gold of swarming sand grains visible only in their beams. Two human voices – the driver and the head of the firing ground – were quarrelling somewhere in the gloom, unable to reach agreement. The driver, a lowly conscript like Alyosha, shouted goodbye with macabre cheer, disappearing into the cab of the vehicle. 'Your commanding officer's deaf! You can yell right in his ear and he won't hear a thing. If you want to, mate, you can swear at him to his face. Oi, Abdulka. You jerk! Bonehead! Smelly git!'

When night had descended on the spot where a moment ago the engine was grunting hotly and headlights shining wanly, all was suffused with loneliness. On the island where a white tower-shaped edifice soared serenely over the dark, resonant steppe with the clarity of a lighthouse, its low, almost ground-level windows glowing and its top crowned with a powerful black-eyed searchlight, two men were left standing: Alyosha, who had just been dumped there, and the savage in his homely old clothing and slippers on his bare feet, whom the driver had mocked in parting.

The stocky unshaven man, who resembled a bath house attendant, or maybe a gravedigger, terrorised Alyosha with his loud and garbled barking as he hauled him into the tower. Kholmogorov found himself in a big empty box-shaped room with a discreet iron staircase that led up to an unlit hatch in the ceiling. It turned out the commander of the firing ground was in a hurry to leave before it got late. It was Abdullayev who had left everything there, but he exploded in anger as if he had found the room in an outrageous mess. And it was all the fault of Alyosha – who hadn't yet grasped that this was where he'd be spending the night. The shell-shocked man clattered into everything in his path and, yelling until he managed to get at least a nod out of Alyosha, he gestured: 'That's where you'll sleep, got it? Tomorrow I'll bring you food, water, bedclothes and soap – got it? Hey, you deaf? I'm talking to you!' Abdulka locked the door from the outside, turned off the light and left. Alyosha lay on his bed as if in a prison cell and only fell asleep at daybreak, when light began to glimmer through the windows, soothing his soul. His commander rushed to the firing ground bright and early, and gave his new worker a wake-up call.

Several days passed. Kholmogorov silently and obediently carried out everything he was charged with by the gruff, shouty man, who at the end of each day would lock him in the castle tower before vanishing. One day while at work, when Kholmogorov addressed his superior from behind and Abdulka failed over and again to respond to his ever-louder calls, Alyosha suddenly realised that the commander of the firing ground could not hear him. He stood for a while in silence, then, overcoming his fear, tapped his shoulder: Abdulka spun around and leaped to his feet with a ferocious look – but then wilted sheepishly upon seeing the bewildered young kid who'd gone limp at his suspicion. And he did his best to comfort Alyosha. 'You and me, we'll be like one soul, sonny. Don't worry, just give me a shove if you need to. I may be deaf, but I'm no woman, you can touch me.'

Kholmogorov merely said, 'Please, mister, could you tell me your name? What should I call you? Do you understand?'

'What's that, eh? What d'you say?' Abdulka started shouting again but when he realised what was being asked, he said indulgently, 'You talk too much – look, who cares? I'm like a father to you. That's all you need to know.'

Abdulka was keen on thinking aloud. Upon hearing the deaf man's unearthly voice, Alyosha would sink into self-pity. *If only I had someone here to talk to*, he brooded. It dawned on him that for his entire service he was doomed to silence – and he sensed reality transforming into a dizzy confusion of mute thoughts and feelings. As he was feeling sorry for himself, something slippery and poisonous entwined his heart like a serpent of temptation: *Look at him hollering away. He's happy enough, while things are lousy for you and they're not going to get any better.*

For a long time Abdulka kept watch over Alyosha, shouting at him, giving him no rest in his desire to haul him through the fire. He heaped him with work, the most futile tasks, to keep the boy from becoming an idle eater, while at the same time rebuking him continually for eating too much: he needed to take smaller portions, put less in his mouth and take longer chewing it. When the month was up, Alyosha gorged on all the supplies hoarded by his superior and was blissfully happy – and Abdulka exulted in being proved right. Kholmogorov grew fonder of the deaf man, powerless to resist that fatherly concern concealed in a man who had first cut back his rations for his own good, then generously doubled them, saving him from hunger.

They had already driven many times around the grounds, which stretched over a good five kilometres of steppe. The firing range began right at the foot of the watchtower. It was empty and desolate, and the whole neatly manicured battlefield looked like a giant open-air replica. A couple of kilometres away, crumbly russet hills obscured the horizon. Every point in this sweeping arena was intended to be pelted with gunfire. It was entangled in a web of communication routes: the slender, sinuous lines of trenches. And in the distance, emerging like a mirage in the bleak steppe, was a toy-like mock town, made up of four prefab cubes and something resembling a town square. All the buildings were three storeys high. The window casements stood gaping like gouged eye sockets. Each pockmark in the walls was charred. The smell of soot hung in the air, although there was nothing flammable in sight. People must have come here to burn things they wanted to destroy, converting them into smoke and ashes.

The firing zones were like pedestrian play areas for children, complete with asphalt tracks and markings that might lead you to mistake it for a complex for learner drivers. Each site had been built to stand alone, like freestanding apparatus scattered around a gym, and they were linked together by still more tarmac tracks.

The thought and attention that had gone into arranging everything against the sterile Martian backdrop was eerily mesmerising. Given the absence of people, it was hard to take in that human beings had created all this – rather it felt as if all the humans here had been carefully wiped out by some alien consciousness with the power not only to destroy but to delete for good while imposing its deadly order. It was as though life existed here much in the way it did in the sands, if indeed that sandy powder was the dust of something living. At the firing ground, only the sand snaked its way across the asphalt paths, slithering right before your eyes the moment the slightest breeze blew in from the steppes. Whereupon your spine would tingle with the realisation that, all around, the sand grains were swarming and hovering over the roads: the vast desert earth was alive. Yet, trained by Abdulka to run things with devotion, Kholmogorov increasingly saw it all in terms of management. On a typical day, he had to sweep clean the tarmac paths on the shooting range and make the rounds of all the facilities. On the eve of target practice, he had to check the equipment and get it ready. And on the days when the soldiers arrived for practice, he would crawl through the trenches on his belly, his face damp with sweat, giving a good bang to any machinery that had seized up; oh, and the three rusting steel dummies that served as bobbing targets couldn't function without him. With his help, the dummies leapt up from the trenches like corpses from the grave, and, if need be, they'd even begin to wiggle on their hinges. At the right moment, the pyrotechnics would erupt and the explosions thunder menacingly.

Immersed in this fun and forbidding world, Kholmogorov felt at times like a phantom. And so indeed he was; only deaf old Abdulka was aware of his existence here. The soldiers in the firing line were oblivious to his presence: little did they know that concealed in the trench beneath the target dummies they were peppering with fire was a living person. Abdulka would tighten up Alyosha's bulletproof vest, put his helmet on him and with a sigh send him off into sheer hell. The moment Alyosha heard the first shots, his heart turned to ice. He heard what the men standing a kilometre away couldn't hear: bullets thrashing into the dummies, crumpling and plopping to the ground like droppings, clinking and hissing. He heard the whizzing as the hail of bullets shot through the air, and his hearing would start to fade out. His soul would sink into the infernal music, shivering in the womb-like emptiness; when an electric humming suddenly ran through a jammed cable, Alyosha's soul would emerge into the world and freeze in terror.

Whenever the machine seized up or the cable lost the traction needed to lift a dummy, Alyosha had to crawl over to his steel friend and use all his might to get it moving again. The firing would cease as the soldiers waited for the targets to pop back up. Alyosha felt as if he had known that pacific silence all his life, with its promise of respite for the nerves, and indeed of a break for the soldiers doing the shooting. The silence was in his power, he was the one who bestowed it minute by minute. But while he worked, his hands continued to convulse as if zapped with electricity, and with each movement his body would writhe in agony: during those minutes, in that silent space, for some reason he was overcome by a fear of death. The men in the firing line held their peace. From their end the soldiers couldn't make out any living soul at the distant targets: when the dummies silently appeared from nowhere it always shook them and stirred the blood. Though the targets would be standing motionless, waiting to be shot, a small flurry of panic would momentarily sweep over the soldiers, and those whose turn it was to fire would be rooted to the spot. From Alyosha's end, things looked quite different. He would be scuttling along the trench on his hands and knees like a hardy little cockroach – and into his bolthole.

There were nocturnal firing sessions too, when the darkness made shooting the targets seem more like hunting. The searchlight beam would roam over the tin dummies, jerking them out of the gloom, and they would flail about as if in a boiling cauldron, bashing to and fro. Bursts of incandescent white tracers from the assault rifles would cleave the blood-tinged amber air of the night. Alyosha would spend three or four hours entombed in his bolthole. It felt as though the entire pack were chasing after him, as if each shot was intended for him – but they couldn't quite make the kill.

After the session, the firing ground would be plunged into emptiness and sleep. The wind blew in fitful gusts, strewing the steppes with a carpet of dust. Alyosha would gather up the empty cartridges – the non-ferrous metal would be melted down and most likely turned back into ammunition – and he'd sink into the silence, like a wild animal. It seemed as if he was walking through the sky as he wandered for days on end across the steppe. He would lie down on the ground – and he'd stay there for as long as he could. He'd get up and push himself to walk on further until he could walk no more. To make the time pass more quickly, he'd make himself food: cook up some soup out of tinned beef and barley, or boil it down into a thickened mass.

When he grew tired of forcing himself to think and colliding with each moment of silence and solitude, Alyosha quickly and freely fell to dreaming, and then he'd roam about the steppes in oblivion. Mostly he dreamed of performing heroic deeds, which always involved offering up his life. He also dreamed of being needed by somebody, or of saving someone. Or he'd imagine it was wartime and he was fighting in a battle, and in this dream he would die saving his imaginary comrades. Engrossed in his dreams, he could skip eating for a day or two, as if he were sacrificing his portions for somebody, and he wouldn't be tormented by hunger. He felt enlightenment and serenity inside, and even Abdulka slipped from memory – food, meanwhile, turned into something intolerable, a reminder of life.

Whenever Abdulka turned up unexpectedly, nothing would change. He would bring some home-cooked provisions, some old newspapers to use as toilet paper, and Alyosha would learn from them of bygone news. The deaf man might have got hold of a radio for him, as Alyosha had once requested, but on every visit he'd rant, 'Oh forget about your crummy old radio, there's nothing worth listening to. Don't go filling your head with all that knowledge, you silly billy! You'll make yourself ill, and that'll be the end of you. You think a bird stuffs its head with knowledge? No, it goes flying on its way, high up in the skies!'

Paternal old Abdulka was aghast that the boy lived without letters. Alyosha never wrote to his family, nor did he get any news from them. Back in the summer, the deaf man had asked, 'Why don't you send your family a letter?' Alyosha replied, 'But there's no point writing, Abdulla Ibrahimovich. It's summer – they'll all be out in the vegetable patch. They wouldn't last long without their vegetable patch.' Come autumn, when Abdulka again suggested writing, he was told, 'But there's no point writing. They're digging up potatoes. They wouldn't last long without their potatoes.' When winter was upon them, he refused to take no for an answer and he sat Alyosha down with a sheet of paper, ordering him as his commanding officer to write to his apparently long-forgotten parents. Alyosha spent a long while gazing at the blank sheet – then he wrote: 'Dear Mama and Papa, I'm serving the motherland, like you told me to, doing my very best. Mama, do take care. Papa, you take care too. I'll look after myself. Bye bye, Your son Aleksei.' Just before New Year, as the holiday was approaching, a parcel arrived from his home region. Abdulka collected it and brought it to the firing ground. The parcel contained sweets, biscuits, jars of jam – all manner of sugary treats. And there was a letter:

Hello Son,

Here's some goodies for you and your friends. Have the jam first or it'll go off, then eat the sweets and biscuits afterwards. We're taking care of ourselves. We've been busy plucking the goats. Looks like we'll get a couple of shawls and about ten pairs of socks. We'll sell them in the winter and that will see us through. We wouldn't last long otherwise. Carry on serving the motherland like we told you to. We're looking forward to you coming home. Eat the jam first or it will go bad.

Abdulka judged how much work to set Alyosha according to the quantity of bread and water he was leaving him – and he would usually time his return on this basis. He would turn up with more water and bread, think up some new chores for Alyosha, unburden his soul in a good old moan about everything and be on his way. Alyosha knew the road that led to the village, but there was nothing he sought from the people there. Their life had become alien to him.

Once a week he had to visit the bathhouse. The 6th Guard Company patrolled the prison colony near the village. Their bath day was on Sunday. Alyosha would arrive early in the morning, walking straight there, and he'd huddle up on the bench near the bathhouse while the company had a nice long wash. They treated him as an outsider, and he suffered gibes and jabs but if he didn't respond, it was because he felt nothing but bewilderment. The voices, the mass of soldiers, the whole hubbub – he found it perplexing, and he'd clam up and block it all out. Slowly the word got around that a deaf-mute was using the bathhouse, and they'd add with a sneer, as though talking about some half-wit, 'He's from the firing ground.'

Were it not for the firing practice, which brought him tumbling down from his celestial walks into the rock bottom of the trench, the peace and contentment might have driven him out of his mind. In the winter, life became harder. Darkness and loneliness were added to his lot. But the frost brought enlightenment, and in his soul arose a tranquillity more palpable than the hunger. Alyosha would clear the hills of snow in solitude, then he'd collapse from exhaustion and fall blissfully and soundly asleep in the warmth of the stove; during the night the snow would heap up again and the drifts grow back, in the same spots and to the same heights, with the same outlines, as though germinating from the same seeds. Inside the tower he would stoke up the stove, though he was sparing with the coal that was so essential to life. When he went out each day to clear the snow heaps from areas that were expected to glisten with a smooth, icy crust like a skating rink before the start of the shooting, he would suddenly feel that without this Sisyphean toil, life would be empty. He would begin slipping into the happy delusion that he was shovelling snow into a furnace in order to stay alive. A sparkling twilight-blue winter palace would suddenly envelop him in a great earthly warmth, to the point that Alyosha would throw off his stifling sheepskin coat, then his *ushanka* trooper hat, and he'd end up bare-chested, solemnly pacing up and down the clean, unburdened paths, believing that he'd warmed up the earth.

During the first winter, a miracle happened: on each new day, he would wake up and start living as if nothing had happened, completely oblivious to yesterday. Everything slid from his memory of its own accord, it burned out in his soul like an ember. He had survived another day, he'd warmed himself up – now all he needed was to keep on going.

A simple command was bestowed upon Alyosha as he was plodding with his sledge along the winter path to fetch bread and water. Fatherly old Abdulka, in his wisdom, had put his motorcycle in storage for the winter and entrusted Alyosha to supply himself with provisions. At the crack of dawn Alyosha would get himself ready for the expedition. By noon he'd arrive at the village. In the kitchen of the guards' company he'd receive a sack of rye loaves and stock up on a full canister of drinking water. For all his other needs he melted down snow, but his drinking supply was always running low and there were no economies to be made. Sometimes he would be left with half a sack of bread but he'd be all out of water. He'd puzzle it over: so, plain old water could be more precious than bread, and it was a good deal heavier to haul – you really had to slog away. Harnessing himself to the sledge, Alyosha cursed at his heavy load, perhaps the way a horse might gently curse a laden cart. If only the horse could know that the cargo was hay, and the hay was to feed his very own self, then wrath would give way to joy. As for Alyosha, he could not rein in his fiery human resentment. It was as if the whole scheme had been specially dreamt up: we'll make him drag his burden for a good fifteen miles, only to dispose of the whole heavy load into his stomach, turning the lot into nothing!

It was here, on this winter road to nowhere, loaded with something destined to turn into nothing, that Alyosha discovered life's simple command. On each journey, his human resentment had been losing its fire. He was beginning to forget that he had in fact been born a human, not a horse. And there came a day when he felt entirely horse, watered and fed for the single purpose of being harnessed to a cart: *Ah, but the whole lot is mine, and it's alive! It's all going to turn into me! My dearest water, my dearest loaves – here they are, warming me and comforting me!* The moment Alyosha halted from weariness to recover his breath, he caught on his numb lips a gentle gust in the piercingly cold air. Sweeping past like a shred of cloth, it instilled in him a hot, damp wooziness. Alyosha stood in the arctic expanse, piercing it like a pivot. Wanting to recover for a moment, he watched everything glitter with a million living snowflakes, while myriad new snowflakes kept on showering down from on high. The sky was frozen and distant: it seemed like a forest blanketed in snow that had been given a shake by something powerful and majestic. And here was a snowflake dissolving on his lips. Alyosha even fancied that he'd seen it whirling down, lonely and doomed, as though it were circling over him in the certain knowledge that it would melt.

An irrational mood came over him. He had spent so long tramping away that now, standing still in the freezing cold, he became drenched in sweat and worried he'd catch a chill. 'If I come down with a cold, it's going to kill me!' Alyosha imagined himself thrashing about in his fever, begging for a drink, and then dying. But with the courage of a child he kept on standing in the frozen terrain, feeling sorry for the dead snowflake. Out of spite for his coming chill, he sat down on the sledge and decided to have a feast: he broke a hunk off the frozen bread and chewed on it, washing it down with icy water from the canister. After he had leisurely eaten his fill, he harnessed himself imperiously back to the sledge and continued on his journey, as though he were blessed with eternal life.

What happened to him that day left an almost physical trace. From that point on, Kholmogorov would often slip into oblivion with a spontaneous smile fixed upon his face. There was something freakish about this smile, like a laughing face slashed with scars. At first when Abdulka saw the smile, it just made him cross, for he thought Alyosha was somehow smiling and staying silent on purpose. Alyosha would come to his senses with Abdulka yelling at him – and he'd be utterly bewildered and confused. Abdulka thought his worker must be suffering from some kind of mental disorder. He decided the winter had affected him, and he calmed down in the belief it would pass in the spring. But the dreaminess did not pass, and the commander of the firing ground began to worry that Alyosha had somehow been concussed in the trench. For some time, fatherly old Abdulka was tortured with the fear that it might be something deadly. He worked himself into a panic: if it was fatal, they'd lose no time in pinning the blame on him; they'd say Abdullayev should have kept an eye on things. But the signs suggested it wasn't fatal after all – and so he decided to keep quiet and pretend he'd seen nothing.

Occasionally, when he could no longer look at that painful smile, he would burst out abruptly: 'Don't be sad, my son!'

Alyosha, however, did not think he was moping.

'Don't worry, Abdulla Ibrahimovich, everything's fine. I'm feeling really good.'

'What do you mean, you're feeling good? What's there to be happy about?' Abdulka asked, reading his lips.

'Well, why not? Am I meant to be miserable? Look around – everything's just great.'

'Have you gone completely bonkers?'

'Well, it's just that I feel good . . . No special reason . . . Just everything's fine . . . '

Once, at the end of summer, Abdulka hurried over to the firing ground during the night and surprised his soldier with the news: 'War's broken out. It's brother against brother.' The deaf man was shaken and frightened, he had rushed to the steppe to take cover, but Kholmogorov simply could not believe him. Abdulka did not sleep that night. Unnerved by the silence and the solitude, he kept on waking Alyosha.

'They've gone berserk. Why can't they just live in peace? What is it they're after? Why do they need a war?' he not so much asked as objected.

'Get some sleep, Abdulla Ibrahimovich,' mumbled Alyosha. 'You just need to fall asleep, and life will pass by.'

But Abdulka didn't sleep a wink; he was waiting for something and he listened anxiously to the silence. There was no war though. On the third day, his disgruntled wife came for him from the village. She was a rather greedy, buxom woman who helped manage the stock with him. She remonstrated and wept, she hectored and shouted, she even raised her fists – and finally she made the fugitive commander come back home.

On the day the order came through saying that Aleksei Kholmogorov had completed his service, fatherly old Abdulka went and climbed into the trench himself and offered his place in the tower to Alyosha. In all those years living in the tower, Alyosha had never once gone upstairs to see where the iron staircase led: only the deaf man was entitled to do so, and he jealously guarded that right, forbidding Alyosha even to peep, always slipping a padlock on the iron door of the hatch.

Alyosha found himself inside a transparent carapace made up of chunky glass panels: he felt like a giant fish in an aquarium. His body had become feather-light, and his feet glided lazily across the resonant concrete floor. From his thick-glassed aquarium he gazed out in wonder, as though discovering an alien new world: chains of humans were uncoiling; massive armoured vehicles were crawling along like woodlice; an anthill of little soldiers was swarming, they were falling out of formation, and the dry seriousness of the drill kept comically slipping from the marching men like loose trousers. Now and then the air would fill with milky puffs blossoming momentarily from assault rifle barrels like tiny parachutes – yet the men doing the shooting sensed them only as an acrid stench.

Alyosha put on his dress uniform and bid the steppe farewell, Abdulka seated him in the motorcycle car and they headed off straight for Karaganda, where Kholmogorov had been promised his eternal steel tooth. The deaf man gasped in shock at the sudden realisation: 'It's all over!'

A NEW DAY IN THE OLD STYLE

Alyosha did not feel as though he had been pressed into service. His new assignment was far more agreeable than he had come to expect from the head of the infirmary, who'd been setting him a steady stream of dreary, repetitive tasks. On this occasion, though, he had been charged with tending to a patient, waiting upon his needs – and this time his assistance did not feel like drudgery. But they wouldn't tell him what was wrong with the strange lieutenant. He seemed sturdy enough on his feet, he could wash on his own, he would slip out into the garden to smoke, from afar it even looked as though he had come to the infirmary not to be cured of his ailment but, quite the reverse, to dwell alone with it, receiving no relief at all. It occurred to Alyosha that perhaps this man was being eaten up by some mysterious disease. Mysterious not only to the patient but to the entire medical profession. This illness allowed him to carry on moving about, eating and smoking, but it caused him distress, which the lieutenant endured in abject solitude, although it was bearable and he could function more or less like a well man.

In the morning, when they brought the canisters of food into the infirmary, Alyosha kept his thoughts on the lieutenant and jostled with the others to get him a nice thick helping of *solyanka*. With his mind firmly on the patient – as though the beef soup had medicinal powers – he reverently carried his gains from the gluttonous scrum at the pot towards the officers' ward. But his eagerness to enter cooled as he knocked on the door and heard an imperious voice say, 'It's open.' Kholmogorov pushed the door gently and stood stock still in the doorway: there he was, at the window in the corner, semi-reclining on the bed in a wide-open gown and slumped against the wall. The man, who gave an impression of profound apathy, did not even look like a soldier. In the vast chilly ward – there was one solitary made-up bed by the window while the rest were unoccupied, abandoned to the whims of fate – a shambolic atmosphere prevailed. The unclothed, flesh-pink mattresses on the empty beds reeked of medicine; there was an almost cadaverous stench. Clean white light poured in through the window, while the window framed a painterly panorama: emblazoned on a canvas of cold and wind were the summer barracks, an oily-green plywood building with fresh timber crosses in its little windows.

The lieutenant eyed the full, steaming bowl. 'Hello, good morning. Here's breakfast,' Alyosha managed to say. The officer did not stir. He had high cheekbones and deeply tanned skin. His entire being was swallowed up by his round, impenetrably dark eyes, which had almost no whites, like an animal's. Alyosha trod heavily across the room, holding the bowl in one outstretched hand and a mug of tea and a spoon in the other. He set everything down on the bedside table. The lieutenant became lost in thought, his eyes taking in only the food. He reached for the spoon, but his hand was trembling as though silently doing something distressing and loathsome. It must have been that annoying tremor which snapped the diner out of his trance. He looked up and fixed a pitilessly greedy gaze on the man standing before him empty-handed. Then, smirking, he suddenly said, 'That's how he was standing.' His voice was commanding, but for some reason he was putting on a hushed tone. Alyosha froze; the lieutenant, though, was apparently waiting for an answer, despite the lack of a question in his utterance about this unknown man.

'Enjoy your meal!' The words slipped out of their own accord.

'That's just what *he* said . . . ' the patient replied.

Alyosha felt ill at ease. The sweetish aroma of *solyanka* soup was drifting through the officers' ward in an insatiable melancholy cloud. In an instant, he came to and left the dying man in peace – he fancied the patient was preparing to meet his end and that was why he was angry with the whole world. But, having made his escape, Alyosha became plagued by an ominous sense of his own doom.

He sat down to breakfast – but the food tasted bad. It was as though something had caused the *solyanka* to turn bitter while he'd been serving the lieutenant. The tea was just as horrible: like dishwater. A malaise crept into his soul. Alyosha sat at the table waiting for something to happen, and he began feeling down. Then he snapped out of it and remembered the lieutenant: he must have finished his food and the dirty dishes would be ready – time to go and fetch them, if the man was still alive.

The sated lieutenant lay sprawled upon his bed as though waiting for his valet. The bowl was empty, the tea had been drunk. Suddenly his calm, measured voice lazily filled the tomb-like ward: 'It all stinks of diesel. Never eaten so much bacon fat in my life. And they call this puke *solyanka*! They make it for breakfast, lunch and dinner . . . Come autumn, summer, spring, winter . . . They serve it all year round. Well, you pillock, don't you feel like heaving yet? Or is it all fine by you? Wow, the way you're looking at me – if looks could kill, now I like that! What's up? You're not happy? What should I call you? Eh? Well, come on, pour your heart out if you like – you can turn the air blue, only say something, Comrade Unknown Soldier.'

Kholmogorov began speaking: 'You can call me by my name, like everyone else.'

'And that name is what?'

'Just a plain old ordinary name.'

'Yes, but what is it?' The lieutenant bristled, lifting himself up onto his elbows.

'You need to stay calm. It doesn't hurt to try.'

'Doesn't hurt? And what would you know about hurting?' shouted the lieutenant.

'I know plenty,' Alyosha said under his breath, trying to control his emotion.

'Idiot!' the lieutenant suddenly said coldly, doubling up as if he'd been jabbed in the stomach. Hissing his words with malice and sulkiness, he went on: 'There's nothing worse than us humans. It's time they shut down the entire madhouse. We shouldn't go on any longer. They ought to wipe the lot of us out. And not one by one, so that someone could slip through the net. They should finish us off all in one go; just press that old button of theirs and solve the problem once and for all. Why are you staring at me with those big round eyes of yours? Come on, man, hop it. Get that *solyanka* down you while they're still doling it out. Well, you won't die from bacon fat – you can't kill a person with bacon fat. But did the pig know whose fat we were eating?' The lieutenant's voice had grown louder and he was sneering arrogantly. He declared: 'Dead men always walk in twos.' And fell silent.

The conversation had begun with a smirk and now it ended with the same formidable emptiness arising out of nowhere. The only thing Alyosha managed to discern in this void was that the stranger had been talking to him as though he knew all about him.

He walked out, feeling he had to be either the deceived party or the deceiver in all this, and trudged down the corridor, with every step conjuring memories of the officers who had passed before him over the years. The firing ground was a place where everyone who handled weapons showed up at least once a year, as if it were some compulsory service. Not all of them stuck in his mind. Alyosha may not have known much about the men, but he would have seen every one of them, at least from a distance. In the procession of faces from the past – all faded and blurry, as though disillusioned with life – the face of the man in the officers' ward made no appearance, or if it did pop up, it was unrecognisable to the point of having nothing in common with the original.

'Kholmogorov! Come over here!' As he carried the lieutenant's dirty dishes along the corridor, still gleaming and quiet in the morning, he heard a shout. It sounded jealous and nervous, and it came from the office, where the door was flung open like a mousetrap.

Whether in abhorrence or fear, Institutov stood hunched in the doorway of his room, holding open the door as he saw out a slight man of eye-catching appearance.

This uninvited guest, who had not even removed his hat, seemed to be in distress. His face had something Tatar, something wolfish about it, and an irate grimace was frozen upon it. His attire had an air of old-fashioned grandeur. The hat, raincoat, shoes and briefcase had evidently been put together as an outfit, and their tobacco colour had no doubt once been in fashion. There was a shirt, presumably once white, and an orange tie with a gaudy flowery pattern, conspicuously exotic in its own right. It remained unclear what purpose lay behind this get-up so unsuited to travel and what had in fact befallen its proprietor. But evidently these items had been worn without change for many days in succession. The dirt built up on the shirt collar had hardened like grime under the fingernails. The coat hung awkwardly from the man's shoulders; it was dull and scuffed, like an aluminium cooking pot.

The troublesome citizen was prolonging his unwelcome presence in the office and, what's more, he was glaring at Institutov as if demanding that he immediately vacate it. The head of the infirmary lost his cool and started to shout. 'Look, I'm fed up with telling you: you'll see him in that wonderful capital of yours! But not here and not now, end of story! You've wasted your time coming here and stirring up trouble, dear Comrade! He'll be shipped out today. There won't be any viewings or changing of clothes, you can do all that at home. You were supposed to meet your son at his registered address, not go wandering about Karaganda in a drunken state. You know, we all die of something or other in the end. I'll die, and you will too – just you wait and see. But I personally don't go running around crying about it, or kicking up a fuss. Now, trust me, what you're doing is hurting your son in the worst possible way. I'm sorry, but you're simply a disgrace to him. Look, what is it you're after? You want us to call the police? You want to sober up in a police cell? Right, Kholmogorov, call the police . . . It's the only way to get through to him.'

The man bowed his head in silence. Then, with a sudden majestic movement he raised his head, throwing a hostile glance this time at Alyosha, but still he wouldn't answer. He just tottered forward mechanically, as though someone had shoved him, then left the room to shuffle down the resonant empty corridor of the infirmary towards the exit.

'Fancies himself the ghost of Hamlet's father!' Institutov said with a snort. 'And in a hat, too . . . ' Then he turned buoyantly to face Alyosha and nodded at the dirty dishes he was holding. 'Well, my friend, you can leave that for today: we have more important work to be done. Come along with me.'

Alyosha did not respond, nor would he budge an inch. As before, Institutov repeated the same old refrain. 'My friend . . . erm . . . erm . . . ' he stuttered. 'The thing is that certain things have to be sorted out, that is to say things are not as they were . . . That's right! Your case will have to be put on hold, it will have to wait, but in the meantime – well, it's just we have some urgent business. It's a matter of life and death. I couldn't do it today, my friend, really, not even if I wanted to. Give it, say, three days, and I'll get to work on your tooth. Nope! That's enough chatter! We still have work to do. We have to – ugh, we have to muster all our strength, knuckle down to work, huff and puff and pull out all the stops. Now listen, you know how it goes, he who doesn't work, neither shall he drink champagne. You're a free agent, no one's holding you prisoner. As they say, you know where the door is . . . ' Whereupon, taking Institutov's advice, Kholmogorov upped and left. The head of the infirmary had a sudden change of heart and raced after Alyosha. 'It was just a joke! I take it all back!' Institutov called out as he ran, bouncing up and down like a ball behind Alyosha. 'My promise still holds! You'll have your eternal tooth tomorrow!'

Institutov finally caught up with him and stopped him, but Alyosha just stood deaf and dumb, staring over Institutov's bobbing head at some point in the distance. Institutov tried fumbling for the right words, seeking out the right note, probing for a chink in Alyosha's armour. His voice was shrill. 'Right, so it's decided! A steel tooth, chrome-plated titanium alloy, all done in a day, without delay, everlasting, a hundred-year warranty! Now, my friend, come on, I'm asking for your help. What'll I tell Comrade Abdullayev? Bail me out, save my good name in this hour of need! Allow me to honour my word!'

The head of the infirmary was straining every sinew to feign helplessness, while endeavouring to ensnare Alyosha in his tooth-pulling grip. For some reason he needed him more than ever. Alyosha couldn't bear to let even a cat suffer. It simply broke his heart to hear the head of the infirmary's plaintive cries about Abdulka. 'And what'll Comrade Abdullayev say?' kept echoing through his soul, as if fatherly old Abdulka himself were lodged inside him, keeping watch and prodding him on. If only Alyosha could have come up with an answer for him, an explanation, but as it was, it would look to Abdulka like he'd just thanklessly run off without the present.

'You've been promising for weeks . . . ' Alyosha began to crack. The head of the infirmary briskly swooped in for the kill. 'Tomorrow, my friend, we'll do it tomorrow! Now what's with all this nonsense, eh? It's your anger talking. You need to know how to forgive. We're all united by a common cause. Just give me one day! Everything's been ready for ages, all that's left is to fit the tooth. Help me today, and tomorrow you'll be on your way home, looking smashing. See, you've insulted me, but I'm willing to forgive all that, and I'd urge you not to make a dreadful mistake. Look, I'm trying to help you, whereas I could have just left you to make that mistake! Oh, yes! Here I am, spending my valuable time and materials on a tooth for you, and you have the cheek to claim that I'm on the fiddle. If you're alluding to the meat that Abdulla Ibrahimovich made me take as a present, then I'll have you know there's no gain in it for me. If I'd done nothing in return, then there would have been. But I gave you an examination, extracted your tooth, did all the preparations for the new one and I'm all set to finish the job off tomorrow. And for the sake of this fine new tooth that will last you for a hundred years, for Abdulla Ibrahimovich's sake, I, a man with a university education, am now grovelling and begging some ungrateful young sod to be patient for just one little day!'

With this drip, drip of words, finally everything went back to normal. Alyosha felt better the moment he yielded. He quietened down and returned to his former self. And it wasn't that he'd been coerced or subdued by this man. No, he was the one who had subdued himself, dropping all his feverish intentions to up and leave this very hour for a promise that he'd be free to go tomorrow. Kholmogorov got ready to depart with the head of the infirmary on this one last job that had been found for him. He put on his dress uniform – now that he'd been demobilised, he had no other outfit – and slipped into his beloved greatcoat which, over the period of his service, had faded to a tawny ochre. The coat had served out its term; now it was looking shabby and made Alyosha resume his scruffy appearance, although anyone catching sight of him might marvel at his seriousness and the earnest dignity that had set like wax upon his face. Beneath its rough, moulting skin, he could feel the unfamiliar coolness of the parade jacket lining, and Kholmogorov instinctively straightened up without realising that all people could see was the bedraggled, faded coat. The hospital waiting room was swarming with soldiers, all doomed to some disorder or other – some had furuncles, others had fresh wounds, others were quite clearly in pain. The whole throng was waiting for the head of the infirmary to appear – and Alyosha waited along with them. He could sense how, any minute now, all those men crowded into the room would have to swallow their disappointment, their despair, even. The head of the infirmary was off on business to an unknown destination, leaving them to wait until tomorrow.

All Alyosha knew from Institutov was that they had a long journey ahead. Institutov had informed him of this with his usual confiding air of importance, intended, no doubt, to take the place of food for his workers. But Alyosha wasn't bothered about where they were heading, how long they would stay or what they would do there. Whatever awaited them, he was shackled to his tomorrow, lost deep in thought, imagining ever more sweetly the remarkable new man he would become. Tomorrow he would be a stranger to everyone. He wouldn't even recognise himself tomorrow. Kholmogorov thought it was what had been destined for all men on earth: to be forever waiting for the next day. The present would never arrive unless you knew how to wait patiently. And that was as it should be, for only tomorrow could be a birthday, not today; it was not ridding yourself of something old that took time, but giving birth to something new.

All of a sudden, in all those poor men languishing with their illnesses in the hospital waiting room, waiting, just as he was, for Institutov, Alyosha saw some courageous cosmic silt, of the kind you might find in turbid water. He was filled with happiness, indeed, he nearly cried aloud for joy: *It will all happen tomorrow! We won't even recognise ourselves tomorrow!*

Institutov turned up. He cast a hurried glance around the assembled men, but nothing too alarming caught his eye, and so he called out: 'For today, my friends, I'll be the pain and not the doctor!' He reassured himself that the patients' lives were not in danger, before having the medical staff politely eject them until the following day. He glanced around again to check that the path was clear. Then he beckoned impatiently to Alyosha.

Outside the infirmary, a vehicle with bulging sides was grazing like a cow, gently chomping on petrol. It was the field ambulance, the regiment's only one, in which Kholmogorov had once set out on his journey, not knowing where he was being taken nor what would become of him. A new driver – remarkably unlike the jolly old wag who had driven him the first time – was sitting self-importantly behind the wheel. Alyosha greeted him, but the guy did not even look round in response.

Kholmogorov was perched in the back like a bird. The seat for the orderly had gone: in its place was a board abraded to a mouldering, polished darkness. It was so narrow that you could easily slide off unless you held tight with your hands. By the door lay some human-length military stretchers and an old, abandoned woollen blanket. It was as though a very tired or indifferent person had just been sleeping on a stretcher in the back of the ambulance and had wrapped himself up in the blanket.

'I've been in this car. It was before you arrived,' Kholmogorov said, thinking that the new driver would enjoy this conversation. 'Piss off!' the latter abruptly replied in disgust, and Alyosha felt uneasy at the gravelly, somewhat whining voice. He could see only half of the stranger's face: the single predatory eye stared keenly ahead. His tightly pursed lips made his mouth look like a seam. The moody man reminded Alyosha of a lizard: most likely he was supple and agile, but none too meaty.

The sullen driver also ignored the boss who was prodding him on. As if by magic the vehicle began to pull away, but so slowly that it was like a boat drawing away from a dock – or perhaps it was a deliberate taunt to the head of the infirmary.

Institutov took offence. 'Look, this is all I need. Life hasn't taught you much, my friend,' he said, with a hint of menace.

'Yes sir, Citizen Boss!' the guy flared up. 'I get mad when people try to teach me about life. Makes me want to put a gun to their forehead – bang!'

'What! Where did you get hold of firearms?' Institutov flinched with fear, then caught himself and fell silent in embarrassment.

But the guy couldn't resist giving still more cheek to the head of the infirmary, who had awakened something evil in him: 'And what gives you the right to preach to me about life, when you do as you damn well please? You'd better leave me alone. I've become all jumpy since I've been in your infirmary: seen too much, I have! Else I might just blurt out the wrong thing one day – well, I only ferry about, you know, undesirables . . . '

'Quiet, my friend, we're in company . . . ' Institutov said under his breath. 'Don't speak out, there are mice about,' he hissed through his teeth and then went quiet.

They arrived so unexpectedly soon that it came as something of a let-down. Institutov leaped out and disappeared into a demure, solid-looking red-brick building. Alyosha peered at the lodge and the double gates, adorned with protuberant red stars. The lodge was deserted, as though everyone had gone into hiding from the cold. Five minutes passed and nobody entered or emerged from the building.

The almost wild expanse of this place rolled out freely in all directions, airy and pure, appearing to lap at the shores of uninhabited granite palaces. Each building was five storeys tall and made of stone, as if it were a castle or palace. And that was how the whole of Karaganda looked, this city built in the steppes. Constructing the city had been akin to draining away the sea. The palace islands and the fortress dams traversed not rivers but the wild-roving river-like winds of the steppe. Every street looked like an avenue: they lay heavy and straight, with the elongated spans of bridges. Anyone who found himself here would shiver and huddle, dreaming of home and pining like an orphan for shelter.

Through the blurry glass everything looked small, as though it had been plopped in a jar.

'See, that's where they decide people's fates, where they search for the guilty. And there's no precision to it. Who knows precisely what he has coming to him, how many years he'll get? The prosecutor doesn't know either; he just pretends to know. If they knew, we'd already be living in paradise – peace and precision, what mighty fine Communism. But I don't buy it. Damn that old Citizen Prosecutor!' the driver said without turning around, gritting his teeth. 'The only thing I respect is the death penalty. You've killed – so die. A death for a death.' At this point he suddenly objected excitedly to himself, 'Well, don't hold your breath, that's the last thing they need! You know, people stink. In the slammer they do, that's for sure. And who do you think they put away? If any of them had brains or brawn, they'd all be living it up on the outside. Who's going to turn *themself* in, or even own up to themself what they've done or thought? But they make out there are some people who smell of roses and others who smell of crap. Those bastards decide who gets a bed of roses and who gets the slops. For certain people to be happy, they need others to be miserable. So, found yourself a cushy little number in the infirmary have you? Think you can spend your life on a hospital bed? You're soft in the head and a weakling, yeah? Or maybe you're a smart guy, a real go-getter?'

Alyosha informed him gladly: 'I've already done my service and tomorrow I'm catching the train home. They've still got to fit my tooth in the infirmary. See, I was looking after the firing range, not putting my feet up, you're wrong if you think that. My place was in the trenches, that's why not many people knew me. Me and Abdulla Ibrahimovich, we took care of the firing. You could say I spent two years at war.'

His words met with mockery: 'Well of course, forward, march! That's where we all come from originally. Smoked weed, seen combat, wound your spilt guts round your wrists . . . '

'Do you mean we come from the same place?'

'Only if they found you among the cabbages. So, my vegetable, you're from which patch then? Pray tell me your name.' The reply did little to calm him down: 'Right, Aleksei, much indebted, cheers for coughing it up. And your father's name, your patronymic?'

'I'm Aleksei Mikhailovich Kholmogorov.'

'Well, that's clear then, you're no relation of mine. You're Rumpelstiltskin, whereas I go by the name of Pavel Pavlovich . . . Got it? It's the name I gave myself and what I put in my passport next to the family portrait. It means Pavel who comes from himself: Pavel Pavlovich. Want to know my surname? It's a good 'un . . . My first name was given to me – but the rest I did for myself. Well, some kind people took it upon themselves to loan me the name Pasha, but I didn't get any further in debt.'

'But how's that . . . ' Alyosha felt afraid before the mysterious Pavel Pavlovich, who, it turned out, had practically been born all by himself.

'It just is. If I say so, then I've decided, and if I've decided, then I do it, and if I don't do it, then what do you expect – I die.'

These words sent a shiver through Kholmogorov. 'Why die, though? If you take your time, you can do anything. That's the whole point of it, of life, that no matter what happens, what counts is you're alive.'

The driver cooled off. 'And who do you think you are? What life are you on about? Wait for what? One man runs about kowtowing and nipping off a bite of whatever falls into his lap. And he's happy, and when his time comes, he'll just lie there on the ground. And the other? He sets himself up, earns his keep, won't give anyone a chance to feel sorry for him and he'll be buried in an expensive new suit. There's nothing he can't do. Even death comes naturally to him. A real man! But it makes you sick looking at the sucker lying with a hole in his head – oh how badly he wanted to survive, he probably screamed. I have no respect for those types. They want to live but they don't want to do anything, and no one's going to come along and make them. See, they've got nothing of their own! Men like that, even their death is a pile of rubbish. It's like the kind of death you'd get on credit.' Then he added in a patronising tone, as though confiding something of importance: 'Death doesn't kid about, and you don't get to joke with it. Each of us only gets one shot at it. Death is like the highest risk game, a game of aces. It's win or die. Make just one mistake, or be down on your luck – and sorry, but goodbye. Everyone's playing against everyone else in this game. The thing I find most interesting is that for some reason the nasty people win the most. There's no precision. Don't screw up your face, no need for that, I won't bite! You're not worried that I'm one of those bastards, are you?'

But Alyosha didn't have time to think, for Institutov had appeared out of nowhere. It was as if he'd crawled over to them on all fours and then suddenly popped up like a jack-in-the-box. His face was pensive, sullen, lofty even. 'Righty-o, chaps. One problem solved. That's grand!' he said, breaking the silence. 'Please note I'm proceeding at my own risk, going it alone, almost groping in the dark. Assistance is nowhere to be had and, as always, I've been left to shoulder everything. Well, let's go, off and away, my friend. To the kingdom of the dead, haha! To the house of mourning and grief! To a place they're not expecting us, but where – ha! – we have a meeting.'

WHERE THERE'S DEATH, THERE'S LIFE

The basement forensic pathology unit extended a warm and hospitable welcome to its guests and service users. It was located at the back of a vast greyish-white clinical complex, through which the weak and ailing were meant to flow like some sort of fluid along the coiled channels of variously sized buildings in order finally to emerge stronger and healthier. The many indistinguishable deserted drives, entrances and exits were all yawning with their willingness to serve as fire escapes and looked, at a glance, like dead ends. They had to circumnavigate this maze, while the same views kept flashing past like a deck of cards being shuffled: the tarmac, a street lamp, yet another drive . . . Pavel Pavlovich steered them patiently through the short and narrow streets. The head of the infirmary elbowed him several times, shouting out: 'You've gone past it! Yes, my friend, there it is . . . Stop! Brakes!'

Institutov got out gingerly and knocked on the resonant iron door. He stood in front of it, alone and vulnerable; he was stooping tensely, his head planted firmly on his impenetrable armour-clad body, and his sturdy stomach peeping from under his green and cockroach-brown officer's trench coat.

The door opened and out poked a smooth, rosy-cheeked mug that recognised the head of the infirmary with a smile. Institutov grimaced in disgust and, gesturing for Pavel Pavlovich and Alyosha to leave the vehicle, he deftly sneaked past the smarmy snout.

The door to the morgue was now flung wide open, revealing a hefty young man, bursting with strength and satiety and for some reason eager to oblige. 'Welcome!' the porter greeted the downcast trio in a syrupy voice. 'You're here for the soldier? Come to send him on his final journey?'

Institutov replied, 'Can we get straight down to business? I'm pushed for time.'

'Oh, but there's just the one. Honestly, it's no work at all!' the porter said in surprise. 'Have no fear. We'll get it done in a trice. You've brought the coffin and suit with you? We're going to make him up?'

'Look, you may be running your own private shop here, but that's not the way we do things!' Institutov bellowed indignantly. 'We have our own rules, our own procedures in these matters.'

'But how can you leave out the coffin? I don't follow you . . .'

'No one's asking you to follow anything. It is none of your business.'

The porter's face fell. 'Well, in that case, you can deal with it yourselves.'

'Quite, that's just what we'll do, and with no outside help, thanks. Could you show my men to the place.' Then suddenly the head of the infirmary named aloud the man who had been on his mind all this time: 'Gennady Albertovich Mukhin. Sent for post-mortem on the tenth of November. The examination has been performed. I have with me the documents from the prosecutor, so would you be so kind as to release the body straight away.'

'Yes, but what are you going to carry him in?' asked the burly man.

'We have everything we need.' Institutov puffed up importantly and, no doubt wishing to rouse his workers who stood rooted to the spot, he urged them on with the poetic exuberance of a team leader: 'Come on guys! Time's running out! Let's have the stretcher!'

Pavel Pavlovich looked around the hall, as though searching for something to assuage his hunger. Alyosha, feeling nervous, clumsily copied his partner's moves as they took the stretcher, allowing himself to be led. The light vanished as they stepped into a dank and gloomy passage, along the bottom of which a draught was blowing as they drew closer to the cadavers. They had to stoop so as not to bang their heads against the oppressive and bulbous skull-shaped vault that disappeared into the depths. The passage was only wide enough for one; two men could not pass. So they descended in single file like convicts. Behind Pavel Pavlovich, all was silent. Alyosha felt underfoot the springy planks that had been laid across the ground and formed little steps; suddenly he tripped on one and stopped dead in shock . . . The stretcher knocked into Pavel Pavlovich, who was still moving forward, and he angrily shoved it back. The strange sensation of this poke in the stomach drove everything home to Alyosha and got him moving again.

The ground had now become rock-hard and reverberant. Something lurking and festering with mould was giving a lively response to each sound. All that the eye could discern in the light shafts was the path they had travelled; now the tunnel began to climb, and a cloud of dust raised from the planks ascended towards the daylight while a luminous spectre of air hovered above, where it was cold and dry. But a moment later Kholmogorov found himself inside the morgue – and what he saw had him wide-eyed in shock. The door opened up like a secret panel: it was as though a section of the dust-coated wall had come away to reveal a hall shimmering with pallid cold bluish fragility. White-tiled walls and floors reflected the flat, lifeless incandescent light so that it cut like a blade.

Kholmogorov had never in his life seen a corpse; he'd never been to a funeral. The hall was tiled from floor to ceiling, with each tile emitting bluish-white light like a headlamp. One half stood empty – for the sake of orderliness – while the other side was packed with wilted waiting naked bodies, also arranged in a semblance of order. Some lay on trolleys: single bodies, or pairs arranged head-to-toe, or piled on top of each other. There must have been around twenty of these trolleys. Mounting up against the wall in the corner was a heap of cadavers that had been unloaded right onto a tarpaulin on the floor and covered with a canvas sheet, but the cover was too short at the edges and lone arms and legs protruded. Through the humming in his ears Alyosha could make out the insistent call of 'Mukhin, Mukhin.' And, instinctively turning towards this call, suddenly he saw the head of the infirmary standing nonchalantly just a couple of paces away, right up close. Merely wincing slightly from the odour, Institutov was quibbling again.

Pavel Pavlovich looked around the morgue with the coolness of an old hand, although not without curiosity. Meeting Alyosha's gaze, he quickly motioned with his eyes, silently bringing something to Alyosha's attention in a brotherly way. The horror subsided, his eyes adjusted to the waxy, anonymous figures, yet Kholmogorov rotated his head from side to side like a blind man and was merely amazed by what he heard. Nearby, two animated voices were cawing loudly like crows, quarrelling amid the chorus of voices keeping intently silent about their own deaths. The abundant human nudity for some reason made Alyosha think of a bathhouse. He imagined this freezing room once upon a time giving off clouds of bathhouse vapours. But in that bathhouse, where people emerged from the steam as naked as babies and shrieking from the whole experience as though they were being tickled, it was blissfully breezy to go without clothes. In this place, not a single one of these lifeless bodies could feel that delicious lightness – they were probably not even human now. Alyosha began to feel odd, swaddled up in his coat and uniform amid all the glaring nudity. His clothes suddenly felt as heavy as lead and he had the repulsive sensation of being covered all over in tawny fur, like a monkey, from the shag of his ochre greatcoat.

'Mukhin, Mukhin,' rang out over and over beneath the vaults of this hall where no mourners were to be found.

In the hall the funeral team was greeted by another porter, who offered his commiserations as if they were relatives of the deceased. It turned out that the hefty man who had met them at the door was the one tasked with running the errands.

This new porter was in the prime of life and looked even burlier than his accomplice. Under the white surgical cap that he wore to hide his bald spot, a rustic face smudged by drunkenness was framed with manly silver sideburns. He must have overheard the discussion between his deputy and the head of the infirmary from down the tunnel, and was no longer holding out for anything much. Institutov quickly adopted the same sculptural pose, only this time expressing contempt; twining his overworked arms into the same toothpuller's knot, he disdainfully proceeded to dictate his duties to the new porter and demanded that he hand over the body of 'Serviceman Mukhin'.

Yet the magnanimous smile, revealing a row of white teeth that resembled pig gristle, was not wiped from the imperturbable porter's face. Feeling himself a true medical professional in his white surgical cap, the elderly man eyed Institutov coolly. 'So, it's Mukhin, you say? No mistake here? It's that particular Mukhin, is it, not some other one? We have to be quite sure, because it's so easy to make a blunder.'

'Here's the sheet! You can see for yourself which Mukhin it is,' Institutov raised his voice, but for a long time his opponent remained unmoved. 'All well and good, of course, that you've got an official paper. And if Mukhin's name is on it, then it's our job to release the body of the deceased to his friends or relatives. But look, you're turning this task of ours into an equation with three unknowns. Unknown number one: where's the coffin? Unknown number two: which one of you is the relative? And the third one: where's your respect for the deceased? Everyone we've got here was caught on the hop by death. They didn't see it coming, didn't get a chance to smarten themselves up; now, where's your respect? That's what we want to hear from you. Papers are papers, and of course they need to be in order. But you see, everyone who comes here has some paper or other; no one's ever turned up and taken a body from us just like that. So that's why I'm asking: you're quite sure we have the right

Mukhin? Who are you in relation to him? Normally we'd only release a Mukhin to a Mukhin. Or else what happens when the Mukhins turn up tomorrow asking for the body, and they're all respectful, and they've gone about it in the right way – and me and Kolya here go off and look for it, but all we find is your paper, instead of their loved one?'

Institutov slumped and went quiet, realising that he was getting nowhere by shouting; these people only grew more impudent the more loudly you pointed out their duties. The porter, who sensed he had beaten the dentist, was also disappointed because there was nothing in it for him. They'd have to hand over the body. 'Look, all right, we aren't greedy,' he said, unable to take the deathly tedium any more. Then he added casually, as if talking about lost property, 'We'll go and look for him.' The two hefty men set to work. They began checking the trolleys in silence, entering their midst as though wading into water. The elderly porter was already in up to his waist. He smoothly separated the trolleys with his hands – which sailed noiselessly apart like boats – and like a diver eagerly scanned the sea of the dead. His workmate was doing the same, but hastily, without flair. The trolleys must have been loaded with the bodies that had been autopsied and were awaiting release. Each corpse had been split open from throat to groin, like gutted fish, and sewn back up afterwards – and these macabre stitches gaped in unheal-able wounds. It was as though these people had been killed all over again – methodically, ruthlessly and, this time, for good. And it wasn't revulsion but horror at what had been done to them that gave rise to something brotherly in the soul, some kindred feeling for each dead person. Kholmogo-rov had a chilling sensation that he, too, was about to die, as they all had, but just at that moment the ghastly voice of the workmate rang out, for he had found the right tag and for some reason was bursting with pride, or perhaps it was surprise: 'Here he is! Mukhin! This is the one!'

The porters wheeled the trolley out into the open space and, with an impressive air, stepped aside to watch what would happen next. Pavel Pavlovich gingerly moved forward. He and Alyosha put the stretcher down beside the trolley – and again they froze, unsure of what to do. Alyosha stared at the floor. Institutov started fussing between the men, urging them on: 'Come on, grab the arms and legs . . . One, two!'

Pavel Pavlovich complained, 'I won't do it without gloves.'

'You're full of nonsense, my friend! I'm telling you as a medical man: there's no risk to your health. As the comrade porters will be happy to confirm . . . '

'Yeah, but the porters are probably getting hazard pay in the form of extra milk. Nothing in it for me, though. I'm not doing it without gloves.'

The head of the infirmary appealed, in a ghastly voice addressed to no one in particular, as if he had lost his way: 'Comrades! Where can we find some gloves? Are there any real professionals in the place?'

The senior porter grinned with a flash of malice, but he took pity on them, happy to know that they couldn't do without him. In an instant some gloves had appeared. Kholmogorov and Pavel Pavlovich laid the body on the stretcher and carried it to the anteroom. There they found something resembling a narrow-gauge track for hauling up their cargo of death. The senior porter chummily referred to this contraption as the 'corpse-carrier'. They fixed the stretcher onto the trolley, which reacted with a donkey's obstinacy. They were having a hard time in the gloom setting its wheels onto the tracks – it bucked, as if struggling against being shod. 'Now what's with all this darkness?' Institutov called out in an agonised voice. 'Can we have some light?'

'Go on, light the place up then, if you're going to shout, only it'll never happen. There are no lights in here because no one's ever fitted any, though why not nobody knows,' the senior porter said. 'Anyway, what do you want to see? Nothing will get any whiter here in the light. Or you want a light to see where you're going? Would be nice, of course, to have a light. But the thing is we've got the public coming in and out. The moment you fit a light they'll nick it if they're being kind, or smash it if they're being nasty. See, where you have people, you'll have light bulbs going missing. The most you can do is stand here with a candle. Well, do you want to stand here with one? Come on, you can take our place, me and Kolya will stand down, we'll hand over our salaries and you can earn your keep here if you want to look after the candle. We're all for mod cons and that, and if we're walking about these boards like blind mice, that's not to say we wouldn't be glad to see the light and have our paths illuminated. Mind, you can always bash your mug in the mud when there's light too – the thing that really matters is what's in your soul.'

They started their ascent up the gangway of planks: laboriously pushing the trolley ahead, crowding each other in the narrow tunnel, hurrying to make their way out, shuddering from the screech of the wheels. It was oppressive and eerie. But it did not stretch on for all eternity, as it promised, lasting rather for just a few muscularly palpable moments. They pushed the trolley forward in fits and starts. It baulked, digging in with all four of its hooves. Each time they heaved, it sent a quivering tension through their muscles. When they broke through into the light, it was like salvation: they became themselves again, feeling such a subtle lightness, such weakness throughout their bodies, it was as if they had descended to earth from the skies. As they were loading the stretcher into the ambulance, the senior porter shouted out, 'Oi, feet first, you idiot! You're carrying a human being, not a log. Show some respect: he's on his way to kingdom come.' Pavel Pavlovich moodily obeyed. They turned the stretcher around and slipped it into the vehicle under the porter's directions, their eyes averted. When they had finished and were ready to leave, Pavel Pavlovich suddenly refused to get behind the wheel. His voice became sulky and strident, like a child's. Then he exploded in a tantrum, shouting to no one in particular: 'You expect me to drive with my hands like this? Been dragging a corpse about, and now you want me to paw the wheel and drive off into the sunset?'

The porters looked on this spectacle with identical smiles, but they took pity and led the men off to wash their hands. They went back the way they had come. The senior porter led them to an inconspicuous door; on the other side they found a cool empty corridor onto which all the doors in the basement opened.

Pavel Pavlovich and Alyosha went through one of the doors – and suddenly they were in a neat and tidy bedsit with a television, a fridge, curtains on the windows, an old sofa and armchairs. Due to an abundance of random objects and instruments hung all over the place, it resembled a workshop. While they washed their hands, the senior porter and his helper were setting out vodka and snacks. 'But where's his coffin, eh? Who's going to bury Mukhin? He's a soldier and all, so why are you taking him like he's just an unclaimed corpse? Me and Kolya were thinking, "Here we have a defender of the motherland." Thought they'd put on a funeral, could be some compensation for our efforts heading our way. Though it's clear as day that it's a murky case, they don't bring them in for forensics just like that. Hey, the cat got your tongue? Come on, let's at least drink to the young 'un's memory. I'll pour you a bit, the boss won't notice . . . '

Pavel Pavlovich recoiled. 'I won't drink to him.'

'What's that? Knew him, did you?' the senior porter pricked up his ears.

'I knew all of them,' he said testily. 'Knew all the men I've driven over here to add to your pile.'

'Well, well, doesn't even want to drink to the kid's memory . . . Why not have a bite then, mister driver-man? Grab yourselves some sausage.' Holding himself with dignity, Pavel Pavlovich went over to the table and picked up a round slice of sausage resting like a medal upon a rectangle of black bread. The long-forgotten smell of sausage hit Alyosha and he swung towards it, but he couldn't bring himself to take a piece. 'And what are you smiling at? That's some manners you have! Your lot have turned you all into wild animals. How can you hate each other like that? And where's the sausage come into it, what's it done wrong?'

'I don't like sausage,' Kholmogorov said guiltily. These words seemed to astonish the porters, almost to horrify them. The junior one almost shrieked in shock: 'How can you live without sausage?'

Alyosha was at a loss for words. The senior porter began speaking silkily and warily: 'Seen too much, hey; I bet he's sick to the back teeth of life, let alone sausage. I get it. And he can't even bear to look at the living. But you've discovered this terrible secret, and you think you've got to the bottom of it? Look at me and Kolya: we eat sausage, we enjoy life – you want to know why? Live life while you can! You've got to eat and drink, love and be happy while you're still alive. Now, when I die, I'll join them on that pile there – and you'll have to put up with my stench for a few days, apologies for the inconvenience. But all of this here is a holiday camp . . . What, did you see anyone writhing, did you hear anyone howling in their death throes? Nah, it's all peaceful and quiet. But think how many people must have prayed for death to release them from their agony . . . So, see, they got released. And you avoid looking at them? That's 'cause you're feeling sorry for yourself, you're afraid. Don't be frightened. Take a look at death, but with respect, with an open heart. Life can be terrifying. It's not the dead we should be afraid of – it's the living. Death might seem filthy to look at, but inside it's pure as a teardrop. And you're wrong, my dear man, to turn your nose up at sausage. It's got a little bit of the meaning of life, sausage has. If you've turned up in this world of ours, you should at least show some respect and savour it. Now, remember that.'

Pavel Pavlovich grinned and took a few more pieces of sausage. 'May I? Wouldn't mind savouring some of that meaning of life for him! I'm rather keen on smoked sausage, I do recall.'

When they had retraced their steps, he finished chewing the sausage and, the moment the morgue door closed behind them, he said to Kholmogorov cheerfully, 'Bunch of greedy, scheming kulaks. "Enjoy life, be happy," they say, but they operate like clockwork themselves. They're fleecing each stiff like it's a sheep, oh, yes! What's there to be unhappy about? Just look at their chubby cheeks. All stocked up on vodka and smoked sausage. That was mighty strange of you to refuse it, seeing as they were offering. You could have tucked in, you know, savoured its meaning.'

Pavel Pavlovich patiently drove them back through the short and narrow streets. Just as they were leaving the maze they almost drove past another ambulance. The head of the infirmary cried out again, elbowing the driver: 'Slow down, my friend! Stop the car! Well, fancy that!' He flung open the door and jumped out joyfully. From the other banged-up ambulance, which had also stopped, emerged an old friend: another military medic, with his arms flung wide.

APPLES OF PARADISE

The field ambulance was wending its way through Karaganda. The head of the infirmary sat silently in the front; Pavel Pavlovich was behind the wheel, with his back to them. Alyosha was busy single-handedly soldiering in a way only he understood. He was doing his utmost, sitting upright on his perch like a guard dog entrusted with guarding something, yet the name of the stranger kept buzzing insistently in his head. The dead man lay sprawled on the stretcher. Two legs stuck out from under the woollen blanket. Those legs . . . they kept on thrusting into his sight. Each one seemed to be saying something – and for some reason they looked as though they were acting independently. There was something intense about them, something powerful, even. Alyosha surrendered to them and stared, unable to tear his eyes away: it was like watching a man drowning, dragged down headfirst, with his arms twitching spasmodically from beneath leaden water. From beneath the dead man's blanket, likewise leaden in colour, each leg protruded as though from water, swollen with the howls of death, thick stumpy toes splayed and unable to grab hold of anything even if they'd wanted to. It seemed as if death itself was speaking from under the soldier's coarse blanket – and

Kholmogorov was by now clinging like a coward to the ledge to avoid sliding off.

They had arrived. An imperious white ship with a thousand identical neat windows sailed through the air, cleaving the cold glassy calm of the parks. Escorting this ship were a dozen smaller white boats. Everything exhaled peace and contentment, even the crystal-chandelier trees looked as though each was tended separately. 'Ah, just smell that air . . . Marvellous!' the head of the infirmary said fawningly.

At a booth near the vast gates that slid open like a stage curtain, some neatly attired guards made them wait a long time. The delay insinuated that you could only get in once you had lost all sense of your own importance and accepted what truly was important: acquiring permission to enter. Finally, one of the security guards swaggered over to the wretched old ambulance: 'Your permit.'

'No, no, my friend, we don't work here. We've come on business. One of our privates was sent here to the neurosurgery unit, and now we need to tie up the paperwork and collect his things.'

'You here for the corpse?' the guard asked bluntly.

Institutov became agitated. 'Sorry, we've come for his things, we took the body from you last week for a forensic autopsy. Today we're having the ceremony, Comrade, and there's a big difference, if you follow my meaning. Everything has to be sent to Moscow today, if, of course, you'll . . . '

The guard turned his back on them and shouted to the checkpoint: 'Vanya, meat wagon's here, let them in!'

Once the vehicle had entered the secure area, Institutov exploded. 'Got themselves a place at the gates of a medical establishment and see how they start lording it up! Who do they think they are, all these unqualified staff? Just who do they think they are? You dedicate your entire life to medicine, all for some illiterate idiot to come along and boss you about at the gate!' Then he stuck his head proudly out into the breeze, let the air blow over him and, emitting a little snuffle, sipped a draught or two of the local air.

The ambulance slowly approached one of the small white-boat hospital buildings – yet even this one dwarfed their sleepy old infirmary. The building had its own private emerald of a garden and was surrounded by fruit trees that had already been prepared for winter. The ladylike apple and cherry trees met the arrival of the cadaverous cargo with a chilly aloofness that suggested they were not cut out for such encounters.

Institutov enthusiastically drew the salubrious air into his nostrils. They entered a reception area filled with cold light. Astride an examination couch, two youthful-looking male nurses were engrossed in a game of suicide draughts, and they were giving the black and white pieces a hard time, delivering them flicks, banging the board and generally doing their best to lose as fast as possible.

When Institutov appeared, the young men quickly quietened down. One of them swiftly sized up the rather short man in his tired old officer's trench coat and boldly blocked his way, asking with studied courtesy, '*Do yu speke Inglish? Sprechen Si Deutsch? Parlez-vous de Français?*' Institutov felt aggrieved but responded with equal courtesy, though he must have known that he was dealing with staff consisting entirely of squaddies undergoing treatment.

'My friend, I'm here to see the head of the department.' The attendant did not bat an eyelid.

'Yes, *natürlich*, go on, I'm listening. Understand? *Verstehen?*' said the talkative young man who had become defiantly imperturbable.

'I'm here about the corpse – I mean the case. If you'd be so kind, young man, I'll obviously need to see your superior this time.' Institutov rattled out his words fairly coolly, worried that the attendant might completely destroy his credibility.

But the young man was in no hurry to answer. He marvelled and, turning not to the head of the infirmary but to his own companion, said, '*Das ist fantastisch!* Georges, the Inspector General has arrived!'

His friend answered gruffly, 'It's my lunch break; I'm not going anywhere. I want some nosh. Serge, pop into the canteen, will you, and get me a bottle of *kefir*. Antonina will give it to you, she's rather taken with you. Oh and I'll have a loaf of white as well, haha! And I'll drop in on Svetlana, rustle up some sugar too.'

'That Sveta is trash, what a filthy girl! And she's grown too big for her boots. We can do without her sugar; let her stew in her own juices. No, go to Antonina, the light of my life, and say, "I'm a fool, a total bonehead, and I'd like some *kefir* please and I'm willing to give you one for it, Mademoiselle." Well, what are you standing there for? We told you quite clearly: go on in, Immanuil Abramovich is in his office, he's expecting you. Goodbye, *aufwiedersehen*, *adieu*, *howdoyoudo*, *buenosdios*, *arrivederci!*'

Outside an office with the name plate 'HEAD OF THE PATHOLOGY DEPARTMENT' sat two more young men – strikingly different from the first pair, in that their noses were buried in a fat medical book and they were deeply absorbed in cramming one of its chapters. But the departmental head was not in the room. Institutov continued the hunt. Wandering around the unit, they passed through the waiting rooms – and again met two young men, who seemed to be filling in for the ones studying outside the locked office. This time, though, the doppelgängers were hard at work dressing the baggy, chalky, clapped-out old body lying on a steel table into an ash-grey general's uniform with gold epaulettes. The procedure was drawing to an end: the male nurses were pulling a pair of trousers with stripes over the deceased man's wizened chicken-legs. When they found themselves in a hall apparently being readied for people to pay their last respects to the general, there they were again: two young men setting the chairs in neat rows in front of the plinth for the coffin, earning tender glances from the weepy relatives of the deceased. All this took place in the comfortable and homely environment of the hall, where the carpeted floor gently muffled all footsteps, as though everyone were moving about in sneakers.

His head spinning from all the walking and the waltz of emotional tension, Institutov floated through the bluish-ultraviolet air. Eventually they came to a room where the walls and floor were lined with tiles: it was evidently a morgue, but one where the snow-white sterility was carefully limited to just a few resting places. The concrete ledges on both levels lay empty. Eight hosed-down concrete racks were attached in two tiers to the walls; the space at the wall with a clean little window was filled by a steel table that shone like a mirror. The young men who kept popping up had beaten them to it again: in the middle of the morgue, oblivious to the world, darting like lunatics from wall to wall, they were kicking a crumpled old shoe in place of a ball. It was clear at a glance that they had set up their own gym in this hidden corner: the iron snout of something resembling a barbell was peeping from under a ledge, and a pull-up bar had been discreetly fixed to the door frame.

This time it was no illusion: the male nurses who had called each other Serge and Georges in the reception area really were here. It seemed as though the young men had been running ahead of them the whole time, presiding over the huge building, having dreamt this all up as a jape, or having invented their Immanuil Abramovich for the sake of appearances.

Their matte bodies, glistening from their footwork and naked to the waist, assailed the nose with the cloying scent of an aftershave that both men had soused themselves in like sponge cakes. And they shared the same coiffure: hair tucked behind the ears, lovingly slicked back and shining with something greasy resembling shoe polish that made their heads gleam in the light like buffed-up boots. The more assertive one seemed to be younger. When one of them lasciviously yelled, 'Go-o-o-a-l,' Institutov, whose presence had gone unnoticed, boomed like a judge: 'As you were, players! Stop your clowning. You'll explain this outrageous behaviour to Immanuil Abramovich. Have you no sense of shame? Fancy yourselves the Brothers Karamazov, eh? Look, I'm pressed for time. I have no intention of putting up with the antics of two cocky little brats.' The male nurses deflated and reluctantly pulled on some blue surgical scrubs that were most likely hand-me-downs from the doctors.

One of them puckered his brows expectantly, while the slighter and slenderer one kept his distance from Institutov, saying coldly, 'We aren't your men. We can only take orders from Immanuil Abramovich. You, Comrade, must have landed from Mars.'

'Comrade Head of Department! Immanuil Abramovich!' called out the head of the infirmary.

The sleek young man grew uncomfortable and hurried to make amends: 'Hey, now why are you shouting? What's worrying you? We'll sort it all out straight away. *S'il vous plaît.*' He gave Institutov a dignified, tender glance – and the head of the infirmary suddenly responded with a mellow sort of smile.

A few minutes later the strapping suave attendant and the pompous toothpuller who resembled a cockroach had developed such a rapport that the two of them were already breezily running things in the morgue.

'Sergei, my friend, we shall need to bring in the body,' said the head of the infirmary gently, talking down to him ever so slightly.

'Don't you worry, just relax,' the young man said in a deep, languorous baritone and, with the predatory gait of a cat, he swept across the morgue to unlock the back door, bearing his aloof, manly face like an egg on a tray. He had a bunch of keys hooked to his belt.

Pavel Pavlovich drove the field ambulance up to the back entrance. They brought in the corpse, still draped in a blanket, and tipped it from the stretcher. The load hit the mirror-like surface of the table. Glancing at the back of the body, all smeared in dirt with its gaunt shoulder blades protruding like chicken wings, Serge yelped in surprise: 'But that's one of our customers! Wow, who'd have thought it . . . Look who's shown up! The fatherland hasn't forgotten its heroes, I see. I remember when Georges and I were called to the operating theatre. Intelligence reported that a soldier had croaked on the battlefield. A stray bullet, could have happened to anyone. And the hero's body never went under the surgeon's scalpel. Haha, Georgie and I weren't in much of a hurry either: we were, ahem, getting amorous with one of the local ladies. So we got there, politely put him on the bier, chatted courteously about culture and literature and fine young ladies before we drove him away . . . And then the customer suddenly comes back – well, I'm impressed, bravo! Georgie, what river did you send this little log down? Forsooth, I tell you, my naïve little *kefir*-guzzler, there are rivers that flow backwards!'

The male nurses were rocking and choking with laughter. They were grabbing each other as though slugging it out, and their lively, happy laughter was plashing about the mortuary. And the moment Pavel Pavlovich growled moodily, 'It's you two that ought to be lying there, top-and-tail,' the young men's eyes popped in delight and, unable to muster words, they fell into another fit of giggles, no doubt imagining the scene vividly.

'Well then, Private Mukhin seems to have left an indelible mark in the memories of Sergei and Georgii,' said Institutov hastily, in the hope that the male nurses would let up. But a new burst of laughter broke out.

Pavel Pavlovich spoke louder: 'Cut it out, you clowns. Or if you like, I can beat some tears out of you. I do love watching men cry.'

Serge instantly quit laughing and spat some words out at the stranger: 'I'm talking for the benefit of people who possess a sense of humour. Georges and I couldn't give a monkey's who this Mukhin geezer was and what kind of heroism he was up to. These Mukhins, they drop like flies, the tiniest thing gets them – and then you're preparing for your next customer.'

'Always prepared!' said his workmate, neighing like a horse, but his friend for some reason cut him short with a spiteful look, and he clammed up.

'So, our Mukhin is your customer.' The head of the infirmary spoke amicably, wanting to butter up the now cagey young men.

'Well, I don't know . . .' Serge replied lazily. '*S'il vous plaît* . . .'

The head of the infirmary continued cautiously. 'I do love a good joke, of course; all this boyish laughter and zeal. I was young myself once, you know, and I wasn't – put it this way: I wasn't afraid of death, I laughed in its face. But as the old proverb goes: if you want to eat the fruit, you must climb the tree. That's enough, you've had your fun. Now it's time, my dears, to get to work. To spruce up your customer. Work comes first!'

Georges shook his head like a stallion and gave a big delicious yawn. Serge spoke for him: 'We can't do it, we're not old enough.' Then he fell into a sulk, drew himself up regally – and suddenly left the room. Institutov did not remain flummoxed for long, for into the morgue strayed a ward assistant, who was being herded along like a cow. She was a deflated, stooping woman in a medical gown that hung on her shoulders like a sack – indeed it looked as though it had been sewn from sackcloth. Serge was still wearing a wounded expression, but he could not resist saying behind her back, 'And please give a warm welcome to . . . the sewer rat! Attired in white. A manual worker. Well, what are you standing there for? Get to work. I'll start the stopwatch, maybe you can set a world record.'

She turned and looked at her herdsman with devotion, mysteriously willing to grant his every wish. Serge evaded her gaze nervously. He had picked up a cassette player from somewhere, all wound up in duct tape, making it look like a cheek swollen with toothache. The noise issuing from it sounded like teeth grinding. Suddenly it emitted a wailing like a stab of pain, then it began whining again, shifting between groans and howls and the gnashing of teeth. The male nurses made themselves comfortable on the concrete ledge, engrossed in their new toy. Serge jealously kept a fast hold on the machine, cradling it like a baby. Crooning away, they were dangling their legs freely from the ledge, as though on a swing, and tirelessly nodding their heads to the beat.

The ward assistant glanced brightly and hungrily in their direction and set to work, moving her arms back and forth as though in a daze, holding a rubber hose in one hand and a rag in the other. 'Stand back or I'll splash you all,' she said with concern, glancing at the strangers with the same child-like simplicity, as though their presence were superfluous. But she clearly enjoyed spraying them with water. All she was after was some attention, to feel needed. Yet the sight of her somehow provoked a feeling of shame. She could not have been all that advanced in years – surely they weren't looking at an old woman? Yet her sagging cheeks, frail lips, thinning eyebrows and wrinkles – even the limp, ingratiating way she spoke – all implied old age.

Having escaped notice while washing one half of the body, she began work on the other side, wielding the hose and rag. She knuckled down, single-handedly rolling the dead body onto its back like a mannequin, although no one was looking her way; then, apparently eager to please, she clucked loudly in sympathy: 'Oh, I can't get this bit clean! The hands are as black as an African's.'

'She's trying to wash off his tan! The silly goose has never seen a tan. Looks like young Mukhin was somewhere hot, been basking in the sun,' said Serge.

'Oh, what a face, I've never seen such a beautiful face . . . ' she said.

'Fallen in love, my little rat? So rats need love too?' said Serge with gusto, locking tenaciously onto her pitiful gaze. 'Well he's still quite a looker: see how much gold dust she's panned out of him. You wanna marry him, eh? Is it love at first sight, or have you had your eye on him for a while?'

'If only old Mukhin had known –' Georges stammered, clumsily entering into the spirit '– he was such a hit with the girls!'

'Ah, it's true love. Now they'll merge in a kiss . . . Bravo!'

'Nah, it's – you know, platonic,' Georges said with a chuckle.

Institutov spoke in disgust: 'Our comrade is hard at work, putting her heart and soul into it. What's so funny about that?'

'They're finding it funny that somebody's died but they're still alive, and they're laughing at her for taking pity on him, when they couldn't care less about a soul,' Pavel Pavlovich snarled, not concealing the fiery dislike in his wide eyes.

This time Serge ignored the stranger – he just turned up the music, until the jarring metal noise drowned out even their own laughter. 'Cocksuckers!' Pavel Pavlovich called out. The male nurses leaped off the concrete ledge: worked up by the music wailing from the cassette player, hunched over and baring their teeth like two angry monkeys, they sprang into action. But their path was blocked by Institutov, whose hands had suddenly developed a special strength: grabbing

Serge in one and Georges in the other, he shoved the men right back onto the ledge, where they landed with their spirits dampened. 'Now, what would Immanuil Abramovich say about this? I don't get it, my friends, are you totally out of your minds? Sorry, but only hardened criminals resort to brute force and vile insults to sort out their problems,' he said, taking fright.

The tape recorder was blaring away. Despite having been beaten back into place, the male nurses were glaring defiantly from the concrete ledge. Serge stared mockingly at his foe, as if giving him the eye, with a deliberateness that suggested he was playing a game. Pavel Pavlovich glowered back at his unabashed laughing eyes, inscrutable as a cat's; it seemed as though they weren't even reflecting the present moment. The young man was getting a kick out of the exchange. Pavel Pavlovich felt an unpleasant quivering growing in his chest, as though a great slimy cold toad had climbed straight into his soul. His eyes started bulging with the tension, and once or twice, against his will, he blinked, unable to pass the simplest test of the game. And each time, the young man blew him an air kiss. Pavel Pavlovich could not hold out and so he gave in, lowering his eyes. Serge continued to stare at him, but now he did so seriously and intently, making a show of studying him, and this caused Pavel Pavlovich torment, as though some other will were lurking inside him, forcing him to submit to this hostile and scornful gaze.

Suddenly a rather lively man, who didn't seem to belong there, looked in on the mortuary. He was on the chubby side, sporting a groomed coppery head of hair and a silky beard that bloomed on his exuberant face; even his intelligent, penetrating eyes – two ripe berries – amply exuded sweetness and the light of nature's fruit. 'Sergei . . . Georgii . . . Boys, keep it down!' he said – perhaps chiding, perhaps chastising, and about to disappear. Silence suddenly fell and the sound of water became audible. Serge and Georges stood to attention, almost bolt upright.

'How do you do, Immanuil Abramovich,' the youth managed to greet him in a sugary singsong.

'Well, look, it's all right, nothing to worry about . . . The ceremony has begun, so can you stay quiet.' And he addressed everyone present: 'Hello Comrades, we've started the viewing, could I ask you to keep it down.'

'Hello,' responded the head of the infirmary.

'Delighted to meet you, hello, hello . . . ' the departmental head said without hesitation, and he graciously greeted everybody present one by one, even apparently greeting the dead man lying on the table amid all the worldly bustle. 'Hello. Hello. Pleasure to meet you. Hello. Please accept my condolences . . . We've begun the ceremony, I'm afraid, sorry I can't be of assistance. However if you wait your turn . . . Sergei, dear, can you keep things in order?'

'Comrade Head of Department!' Institutov pleaded. 'Just one question?'

'I'm afraid the ceremony has already begun. I shan't be able to assist with the removal of your body, it will have to wait, nothing I can do about it . . . '

'Oh but you can help, you can! One of our privates was on your books some time ago – we have the body right here. I'm taking the body back now, but there's still no sign of his things. They should have been delivered to you – well, how can I put it, what are we to dress him in for the occasion? All his things are still on the books in the place where he was serving. His dress uniform, his tie, shoes – everything needed for the ceremony. You were the ones who recorded the fatality – well, I should be picking him up in tip-top condition from you. I'm sending him to Moscow! At zero hours twenty-five minutes. Any delay, if you'll excuse the pun, will be the death of me!'

'Yes, yes, colleague, I understand . . . Sergei, look, could you give out – ermm, a smart set of clothes, I believe is what we need. Now, help out our guests.'

'What splendid words! You're my saviour, Immanuil Abramovich. See, I've also got to drive out to the back of beyond for the coffin – that's coming from another establishment. And the train won't wait – get there one minute late and that's it. Toot-toot! It'll arrive in the capital with an empty space. Oh, how soulless this all is, such a bundle of red tape! You'd hardly call it rational – everything in different locations, and there's just the one of me! Just think about it: here I am, a man with a university education, weighed down with medical knowledge – and I'm chasing about doing the devil knows what, instead of treating my patients, saving lives, doing good! Just think what I have to deal with every day . . . In the infirmary, where you'd expect some semblance of sterility, they defile every square inch of the place. Steal everything they can eat. Spoil everything they touch. And that's just the mice! After these latest developments in the country, one doesn't know what to live for any more, what the future will bring . . . If you ask me, it's all going to hell in a handcart.'

The benevolent man shot Institutov a gentle, understanding glance: 'Now really, my dear colleague, you ought to take it easy . . . Look how pale and drawn you are. Being in healthcare isn't a career, it's a matter of body and soul. But

I can tell you this from personal experience: the only way to treat depression is by communing with the beautiful.' And he withdrew, almost whispering to them, as though they were children: 'Goodbye, Comrades, please do keep your voices down.'

The head of the department vanished in a cloud of his own heartfelt warmth. For a moment, a resounding, primordial silence reigned over the basement. 'Hey, didn't you hear what he said? Chop-chop, go and fetch his things, you ass. Pronto!' Serge hissed at the perplexed ward attendant, who had been stealing time on the quiet, trying her hardest to please him with a new world record.

'Wh-wh-where are his togs, y-y-you r-rat?' said George suddenly in a strangled voice, the veins on his neck swelling up like a bull's. The woman cowered and threw the hose to which she'd been tethered to the floor; bruised by their words and forgetting the soapy rag she held in her other hand, she rushed out of the morgue. Once she was gone, the young men recovered their composure and began chatting away as if nothing had happened. They seemed to be lingering simply to mess around.

Funereal music was leaking through the walls. The mellow, muffled sounds were drifting around like shadows. The ward attendant slipped back in unnoticed, looking like a restless ghost. She had brought into the morgue two thin but well stuffed pillowcases. Institutov grabbed the fatter bundle, shook its contents onto the bare concrete ledge and froze: out tumbled a soldier's tunic that had faded to a greyish hue and some useless old trousers of the same shade. They had been laundered, gone through a good clean, but a pale reddish-brown stain across the entire breast of the tunic still showed through. From the other pillowcase Institutov pulled out a pair of clunking combat boots, on which sparks of blood had caked into stains like burn holes. The head of the infirmary flung aside the blood-stained boots, grabbed the tunic and gave out a whimper, clutching the tunic in his hands as if it were his own doomed soul: 'What's this, Comrades? There should be a dress uniform on their books . . . '

'It's what it looks like: a complete screw-up, sir,' said Serge with a smirk.

'This is the end . . . Oh, what have we come to! They've fouled things up over and over!' The head of the infirmary whined and groaned like a man who'd been robbed. 'The murderers . . . The morons . . . I have to send him to Moscow in this!'

But Serge spoke in a buttery voice, oozing sympathy: 'Oh, so they bungled things a little? Well it happens, we all make the occasional mistake. I can see the perfect candidate, just a stone's throw from you: gormless old cloth-ears here. Go on, take it, a full dress uniform just waiting to be used, and, as for Georges and me, oh we won't breathe a word. We're civilised men, Georges and I . . . Heh heh.' He looked straight at Kholmogorov, snickered and said pitilessly, staring him in the eye: 'What you gawping at, greedy little peasant? Physical fitness uniform, pronto! Man is a friend to man – now, do as you're told.'

Institutov turned in bewilderment to Alyosha and immediately flopped to his knees, wailing: 'Kholmogorov, my dear son, save the day! Let me have it! You'll get an even better one! Tomorrow we'll drive out to the supply warehouse and you can pick out the very best, the very finest!' He began clinging like grim death to the skirts of Alyosha's coat, as though he were trying to snatch off even just a tuft of it, and shook him from side to side. 'Get undressed, come on, time to toughen up,' the male nurses joined in gleefully from behind Institutov.

'Well, what are you waiting for?' Institutov was getting worked up, hearing the mocking, grasping voices behind him as though from somewhere above. 'Give it to me now and tomorrow you'll get an even better one. Look, I can't use my own – I mean I'd happily take it off and use it but they'd see straight through that, Kholmogorov! Now, where am I going to find a soldier's uniform? Where, tell me? I'll scrub the boots clean, I'll do it myself. Just think about it: how can they bury the soldier in my clothes? Don't you feel any pity for your comrade? Just think what it will be like for his mother and father seeing him like this, put yourself in their shoes – imagine it's your own mum and dad finding their son in this state!'

Kholmogorov came to and began handing over his things one by one, to the head of the infirmary's delight. Institutov caught the items and passed them on like hot potatoes to the ward assistant, who lost no time in dressing the other man. Alyosha was standing there shirtless, while she was already buttoning up the shirt on the other soldier, struggling to slip the tie over his head until soon enough everything was concealed beneath the green of the uniform. Kholmogorov had given up his parade jacket, his shirt, his trousers, socks and shoes, and now he was barefoot and in his underwear. Pavel Pavlovich turned away so as not to see him. The head of the infirmary didn't have the heart to tell the shivering half-naked youngster that he couldn't remain like that either.

The ward assistant suddenly recollected something: 'No need to be squeamish, my boy: it's all as clean as can be, all nicely laundered. And I'll bring you some shiny boots, even better than your old ones! I've got some, I have, been keeping them aside specially for you. And we'll make you some footcloths. We can use some old towels, we'll use waffle-weave ones if you like them nice and warm, or if you prefer them soft I can tear up some old sheets.' And she slipped out to get the boots. Kholmogorov was touched by the sisterly warmth in her voice and he obediently began to put on the dead soldier's uniform. 'Right, now we'll wrap you up in your overcoat, and everything will be just splendid!' said Institutov buoyantly. 'It's called making something out of nothing. Well, what did I tell you? Ah, look, your boots have arrived . . . ' The smiling ward assistant came running into the morgue, out of breath, hugging to her chest a pair of weird and wonderful boots that were indeed shiny; in fact they looked like they'd been coated in varnish.

'Phew, ran as fast as I could! Here you go, young man. Have no fear, they're spanking new boots, see how lovely and shiny they are. An officer used to wear them for playing his trumpet in the orchestra.'

'Playing his trumpet? You mean popping his clogs!' Serge said.

The woman got angry and, for the first time, her pale and homely face grew flushed. 'Don't believe him! It's all lies!' She suddenly flew at him in fury, pressing the boots hard to her chest, as though she wouldn't part with them for the world. 'That man got better and left. But he forgot his boots. He had lots of pairs. These were the ones he wore when he played in the orchestra.'

Everything felt new and fragile. In the morgue they were all waiting and waiting for the nearby ceremony to draw to an end; its reverberations roamed about like ghosts, one moment humbly dying away, the next surging proudly like waves in the ocean. The noises drifted through the silence, automatically tingeing it with sorrow, until the male nurses could no longer sit still on their ledge and they began acting out this very grief. They stood guard either side of Mukhin, all decked out in his dress uniform, pulling grimaces as they called out, 'Farewell, Comrade General! We shall always remember you, Comrade General.' Their horsing around once again unsettled the head of the infirmary, and he tried to put an end to it. 'I don't expect Immanuil Abramovich would approve of this. Young men, this isn't the circus.'

The nurses simply looked surprised, but they went back to sit on their boring old concrete ledge. 'Are we disturbing anybody? I mean, they can't see us or anything,' Serge said with a puzzled look, but the head of the infirmary took this as another taunt and remained sulkily silent. In no time the young men were at it again, jostling each other, competing to see who was strongest and shoving each other off the ledge. Finally the last strains of music died away. Institutov began impatiently counting the minutes. Then came the sound of the funeral procession driving away.

Serge and Georges became cold and guarded now the party was ready to depart, and their entire demeanour urged their tiresome unwanted guests to make for the door. Pavel Pavlovich called Kholmogorov over; for some reason his voice was agitated. In his hurry to leave the place, Institutov even tried to help raise the costumed corpse onto the stretcher. 'Complete barbarism. It's all so brutal . . . ' But he suddenly faltered, upon spying the blackish caked-up hole in the dead man's forehead. 'Stop!' he shouted and began nervously rummaging in his coat pockets until, relieved, he pulled out what he'd been looking for: an ordinary first-aid plaster. Institutov peeled off the white backing tape and, with an unfeigned look of anguish, he stuck it over the dark hole in the corpse's forehead. 'There, we're done. My conscience is clear. I've done everything in my power.'

As they began lifting their load, the ward assistant crept up to Pavel Pavlovich and into the gaping pocket of his padded jacket she slipped a huge firm round apple that she had been clutching as though it were a cobblestone, then she ran straight off. Harnessed to the stretcher, in all the commotion the object of her affection did not even feel what had happened. The woman wept silently once she had run off a little way. Then she swivelled her head from side to side, gazing at all their faces and believing she liked what she saw. But the male nurses would not let her out of the building, keeping her hidden away with pokes and prods, and they themselves vanished into hiding like wild little animals, silently locking the door from the inside. 'Georgie Porgies, japers and jesters, jammy little buggers, may they all be damned!' Pavel Pavlovich chanted his incantation without looking back.

DWELLERS IN THE DUST

'All a man has is his mother's belly – that's his God-given protection and shelter. But once we've been chucked out into the world awaiting us, we spend the whole time trying to dive back into that little den. In this world we're given all we need for life – it's only that dear old mummy's tummy that's missing. See, when you're in your mother's belly you're all swaddled up, but once you're out in the world you're hardly swaddled, are you? So there you have it. Birth, my good man, is what frees us all, starting with our little arms! God creates us unfree, and then, because of our original sin, we all get released. And like we're trying to save ourselves from sin, each of us off his own bat begins building his own little house, his own den, his own prison, but we're wasting our time. Now here it really is all the work of human hands – those little arms that were all swaddled up. Argh, those damned sinners' hands! Truth is those houses of ours won't protect us. They're just like sunflowers, where there's evil in every seed. What is it we covet and envy? Our neighbour's house. Where is it we're at each other's throats? In our own homes, where we're jam-packed like sardines. The Earth is ginormous, but people never have enough space, they're always pigging away till they choke. They hang icons in their homes, so I hear – see, that's all so they can lay the blame on God, while they're ruling the roost in their own four walls. You think God's going to punish them? Well He ain't. Yes true, He is the creator, but how can His handiwork be guilty before its maker? I mean, how can this object here be guilty before me, and what comeuppance can it expect from my hand? Say my own handiwork gets me all worked up: I can't even burn it, because I wasn't making it for myself, I was making it for the grave, and it stops belonging to me the moment I hammer in the last nail. Well, it's the same with God – we stopped belonging to Him after Adam and Eve. When we became free and sinners! He had a son, created him for Himself – and that son belonged only to Him. Poor thing, he suffered on the cross. Deary me, how he suffered when the Creator was driving the last nails into him for the perfection of human life. But He didn't drive any nails into us, did He? No, my good man, everything the Creator made that wasn't for Himself is beyond the reach of His hands. And no matter how much of your heart you put into your handiwork, you always know where its limits are. However much you invest your soul in it, your soul's not going to be eternal if what you're investing it in isn't eternal. Now, I believe God Himself is made out of eternal stuff – He's not made out of these here planks. But it's only if you've created yourself that you can create thousands, millions of eternal beings just like you. But from the look of it, God can't create more beings like Himself, because He doesn't possess the secret and He wasn't created for Himself but for us, for humankind. And that goes for people, too – they aren't created for themselves, they're created for their children. Right, and what do we need all this for? Sorry, my good man, but it's not for me to say. I'll just slog away my time. I'll make myself a coffin for my final journey – now that's where I'll invest my entire mortal soul, oh yes! I'll brush it all over with varnish, line it nice and soft – it'll be as comfy as snow – and then it will be good night, Pankraty Afanasevich, sleep peacefully. God never let me have kids. That's the fate He chose for me: not to have any children, my good man. Because I have so much bountiful soul in me, beautifying my coffin will be like ascending up to heaven itself out of sheer happiness. And I'll be flying . . . See, the moment I sense my death is near, I'll set to work. It won't be like making a coffin, honest, it'll be like creating wings! And who'll begrudge me? Nobody! And what will trouble me? Nothing. They'll close the lid behind me like it's a door. They'll leave me alone and in peace – and then it's into the earth, into my own dear grave, as good as going back into my mother's belly . . . Something happens after a person dies, only it's not Heaven or Hell, and the Lord won't breathe a new soul into you to replace the one that's given up its heat. Maybe in our hour of death we depart for another creator, eh, my good man? To one who doesn't hew us out of flesh but creates us out of dust. That one who breathes something into our dust is another creator, that's right. Not a carpenter but a herbalist, that's how I understand it. See, the only thing that grows out of those grave mounds is herbage. And what's herbage for? It's for everything – medicine, food, shelter for the bugs, and it's just generally teeming with life . . . Now this herbalist must be the one who decides which of us gets to be which herbs or grasses and which of us turns into food for the worms . . . '

The Herculean grandfather craftsman cut an imposing figure: he was bearded, with a great round forehead that swallowed his hair right up to the crown of his head, which almost formed a second forehead in its place. He held forth tirelessly while lovingly embracing one or another of his robust heavy-shouldered coffins that measured a head taller than him.

The coffins stood in rows, leaning upright and silent against the walls.

In the middle of the timber shack, in the windowless space where the dirt floor was trodden down by boots, the craftsman's latest work lay like a ship on the stocks: it too was a coffin. This was the handiwork of which he'd spoken. The unfinished coffin seemed much more solemn than all the completed ones and it looked particularly impressive amid the other unremarkable upended caskets. The gates of the shed were flung wide open, revealing a sombre grey sky of tufty clouds. One of the gates was entirely lopsided and supported by a post, like a one-legged invalid leaning on a crutch.

Near the entrance lay a heap of boards that had once been fencing, wooden walkways and plain old timber crates. Not a single board was clean; all were plastered with mud, battered and caked in clay. These planks were as mucky as swine and furry with thick bristles; they had splinters visible even to the eye and looked as rough as a pig's snout. But it was clear that whenever the craftsman fished out a board from the pile, set it on the workbench and lovingly ran his crude plane over it, each plank would be purified of sin, take on a tender hue, almost the colour of flesh, and turn as smooth as a human palm, with all its unique natural lines laid open to the eye.

For this reason the workshop did not smell of rot or decay.

It smelled of life-giving wood resin; the freshly-planed boards nailed together into coffins exuded the kingdom-of-heavenly spirit of pine and spruce.

The craftsman was searching for a suitable coffin, one that fitted in size and most likely in rank too. He went to take the measurements himself, although Institutov, in his desire to get everything going as quickly as possible, had already issued the prison-camp worker his orders, informing him what rank of coffin was needed and dictating the precise dimensions of the deceased. 'But he might have swollen . . . Might have shrivelled . . . Depends on what kind of man he was, a good or a bad 'un.' Then, disregarding the commander, and walking openly and upright as though on stilts, he went over to the army field ambulance that had been driven into the prison camp, unarmed and clapped-out from its long journey – quite unlike the trucks that came in from the outside world, which were stuffed with living creatures under guard. The ambulance had not waited for permission to enter but had simply sailed into the barbed wire zone more breezily than death itself, doing nothing at all to disturb this dingy world, and waved in by the guards without the slightest inspection.

The coffin maker peered into the back of the ambulance, his gaze dwelling for a minute alone with the corpse. Then, when he had gone ten paces back towards the workshop, he said gravely, in a reproach that only he understood, 'He's withered.'

Institutov stood there, arms hanging by his sides, and watched this perplexing prisoner walk back, realising in amazement that he was now dependent not only on this man's labour but also on his opinions. 'My friend, how much time will you need to carry out the procedure? Will one hour be enough to get it done?'

'For the love of the Lord, Citizen Boss. Work steams ahead when your soul harbours no sin. It all depends on God's mercy: it could take an hour, or, for our sins, it could take five.'

'You know, I can't afford to wait for mercy from your God. See, your personal sins are nothing to do with me; religion is just an invention for slaves. That Jesus Christ of yours would have been better off learning to read and write before teaching morality to all mankind.'

'So then, we have the coffin, the fabric covering, the zinc plating . . . And seeing as you don't believe in God, you can throw in a packet of tea, and I'll do the finest tip-top job, like a bespoke order.'

'Well now, we'll talk about your compensation when we've seen the end product.'

'Ah yes. Then you can slip me another packet on top of it, Citizen Boss. And some sweets to go with the tea. That way I'll be certain to do you a coffin within the hour. You can find it all in the shop. See it's us folk who are lowest in the food chain, I'm afraid. When our time comes to die, we'll find it easy – 'cause we've got nothing. Go on, give us the payment up front, to keep my inspiration up, otherwise my thoughts will drag me down.'

Institutov sent Pavel Pavlovich off to the shop. He waited impatiently until he'd returned, then showed the craftsman the two packets of tea and the biscuits, hoping simply to lure him into work, but the coffin maker refused to speed up without an advance and the head of the infirmary gave in, powerless that whole day to compel anyone to do as he wished.

'And what about us – we meant to live on air?' Pavel Pavlovich bellowed.

'No, no, of course not!' Institutov took fright. 'I'll see that you're all fed . . . I'll go to the canteen and arrange it right now!'

Pavel Pavlovich was content. 'So he's out of sight. Huh, could have brought us a hunk of bread . . . Well don't hold your breath. You think he'll bring it, seeing as he's hungry himself?' He looked Alyosha over with a smirk. Kholmogorov resembled a looter, in his moulting ochre coat, the corpse's tunic missing its white lining at the collar, the lacquered orchestral boots, which were pointy like a pair of ladies' heels. Pavel Pavlovich said in a melancholy singsong: 'Hey, Commando, loosen up. So you're wearing a dead man's things; so what? You're alive.'

Alyosha hovered at the entrance to the shed until the craftsman called him into the warmth and began talking to him as he shifted his coffins. It turned out that deep inside the workshop, sitting alone on a stool, there was another old man, bespectacled and beardless but in all other respects a wrinkly copy of the man who was single-handedly shifting the coffins. This man had the same shape of bald patch on his head and he too was dressed in a padded jacket with a number on the chest, but even without that, his entire physiognomy showed him to be a prisoner: he kept a grave and resolute silence, the kind that expresses either agreement with everything or complete denial and dissent. His lips were closed tight and puckered, as though he was about to spit. His plastic glasses were bulky and resembled fish bowls, and the cantankerous old man's face had something of the aquarium about it too: his eyes were two colourless little minnows, his moody lips looked like a snail and his shaven cheeks were all wishy-washy. His lean, lonely figure was bent into a question mark so that his large balding head fell onto his puny chest. He was sitting like a schoolboy with his legs tucked under the stool and his elongated shrivelled hands on his knees. But when the bearded craftsman had finally picked out a coffin suitable in all respects, hugged it like a child and carried it over to the workbench, the prisoners began squabbling about God, whom the coffin maker kept on stubbornly bringing up – and the shed shook from the din.

'Our homes, those little dens of ours, they're full of fear. Oh, why did our dear mothers bring us into the world, may God forgive me, if all we're ever doing is looking for a place to hide, trying to get back into that little den of ours . . . Amadei Domianovich, what do you make of it all?'

'Disgraceful!'

'If you say so, Amadei Domianovich. I bow to your fine intellect, the nobility of your soul and your squeaky-clean conscience, but it's just your pride that's talking, my love. You practically live here; you sit in the corner on that stool spitting at everything you see. I don't know what it is you're eaten up with. So we've done a lot of people in, well let's at least try and rescue our own souls.'

The frail old man's teary eyes flashed piercingly and he pursed his lips even harder and more disgustedly than before. At that moment, the coffin maker turned around, looking straight ahead, and banged into Alyosha. They found themselves so close to each other that it was as if they were comparing heights: the burly old man barely came up to Kholmogorov's shoulder. Cutting straight through his forehead was a scar that looked as though it had been gashed out by a giant chisel. The man's diminutive size and the close-up sight

of this tender-as-a-baby scar made Kholmogorov's heart ache
with involuntary pity. The craftsman looked up in surprise
and immediately marvelled, his face brightening and opening
up: 'Oh what a strapping young man! Seeing as you're so big,
you can give us a hand. My assistant's gone on strike, you
see, but don't get the wrong idea, son – there are only one
or two minds like him on the entire planet. They brought
him to me from the barracks as a scraggy little body wanting
a coffin. The doctor had certified his death. I began putting
him in the casket – when suddenly he was alive! He looked
at me like a saint, all disapproving, then he puckered his lips
and spat right in my eye. I don't know what kind of force
was at work, but it just so happened, miracle upon miracle:
the guards got tired and popped outside. Right, so I quickly
slipped some bricks into the coffin, nailed down the lid and
hid Amadei Domianovich in another coffin I had here – and
I nursed him back from the brink till he'd mended. This
whole time he wasn't talking to me; all he'd do was look at
me like he was wagging his finger. He wore me to a frazzle,
I confessed all my meanness to him. Later, though, he found
his voice. And how finicky he was! I fed him with a spoon, and
he'd only have warm food, so I gave him warm herring – a
delicate constitution. When he was pulling through, I tried
to drive it home: you've been through death, you should
consider yourself blessed with eternal life; now stay here in
this coffin, live and rejoice! But he wouldn't have any of it,
too proud he was . . . He sat on that stool in the corner and
refused, so in the end we got spotted and they added to his
sentence and he'll never get out now. They treated it not
as an attempted escape but as making preparations for an
escape. But I'm happy: me and Amadei Domianovich, we're

birds of a feather. I'd be lost without his opinions, like a lid without a coffin. No question about it, we're like soulmates. If it hadn't been for me, he'd have rotted in the ground ages ago, but because of me he's risen from the dead!'

Kholmogorov had the sensation that he had experienced all this before – both this kindly old man with his broad forehead and the very same story about a man who was dead and suddenly came back to life. The coffin maker called him over to help: 'Hold the coffin for me, son, while I nail the fabric to it. Hold it nice and tight and turn it the way I tell you.'

The lids for the coffins lining the walls had been taken off and slipped like coats or jackets over the caskets' shoulders. Alyosha began to grasp that he was helping the craftsman and his face lit up: 'Tomorrow, Granddad, I'll be catching the train and going home. I've done my fighting . . . '

'And what war was that, son, that you were fighting in?'

'One where they were firing at me with assault rifles, sniper rifles and RPGs!'

'Well then, God bless you, keep up the fight. Now, can you turn it on its side. Ugh . . . Look at the cloth they've given me. You can't stretch it taut: it needs darning.'

Before their eyes, the smooth-planed stray boards that had been knocked together were swaddled in red fabric. The craftsman gently strewed the bottom of the coffin with shavings which he scooped up from right beneath the workbench. He ripped an old white bed sheet in half, fiddled about with it, hammered it in place, and Alyosha saw within the coffin something resembling a featherbed that was raised at the head. But the moment the last nail had been driven in and the remaining folds smoothed out, the coffin became lifeless and all the good work done by human hands took on a different cast: the quilt of shavings on the floor of the coffin grew stony; the beautiful smoothness of the cloth began to torment the eye.

The craftsman went out and, a few minutes later, returned with a trolley carrying a long box made of dull metal that looked like a large trough. He lowered the still empty coffin into this box as though into a pit. 'Amadei Domianovich, can you get us a fire started, stoke up some embers, while we put this new one into his coffin. Well, what can you do? He won't say anything – he's on strike! All right then, I'll do it myself, and you, love, can go and call one of the guards. Tell them Pankraty Afanasevich wants them. They need to come and inspect what we're putting in the coffin. Ugh, I wouldn't mind jumping in there myself, God forgive me . . . And can you give your boss a shout, the client, wherever he's got to. There's still a packet of tea owing from him!'

Pavel Pavlovich set off to find the head of the infirmary. But he couldn't have given a hoot about listening to people, going anywhere or doing anything: slipping his hands deep into the pockets of his padded jacket as though feeling chilly, he casually went off into the drab haze, like a sailor pacing about on deck. The prison camp – hungry for human lives, bristling with row upon iron row of barbed wire and cut through with narrow paths spread so thickly with gravel that as his boots trod on them, they twisted in with a crunch like screws – did not frighten Pavel Pavlovich. It didn't even jangle his nerves, which were suddenly as muffled as the gravel beneath him. He soon returned and in a strikingly different mood. He was greedily and rapturously gnawing on a large firm green apple. As he did so, he was wincing and clacking his teeth; the apple was so sour that he even sucked in his cheeks. But he tolerated it – and he chewed and chewed, clearly delighted. 'I put my hand in my pocket, and there was this apple! It was like it dropped from the heavens into my pocket! Must be about three years since I last saw an apple close up. You don't believe me? I swear on a loaf of bread!' he burbled loudly with his mouth crammed full, acting as though he'd gone deaf. 'Here, go on! Take a bite, you skin-and-bones! It'll bring you luck . . . Take a bite, it ain't stolen!' And he bossily thrust the fresh juicy half-eaten apple at Alyosha. Kholmogorov smiled, so as not to offend, but, dodging the apple, he offered a cheek instead of his mouth and so the fruit slid across his face, leaving a damp and oddly pink frothy trail. Pavel Pavlovich had bloodied his mouth. Perhaps he had bitten his lip or his gums were bleeding. He laughed indulgently at himself when he real-ised that he had injured himself on an apple, and that very instant in one slick movement he drew from inside his boot something resembling a knife: it was an iron spike that had been flattened and sharpened, around the size of a pencil.

A short distance from the shed, already puffing and belch-ing smoke into the wind, was a hot fire that had been kindled in a tin tub, posing no risk to the workshop. Pavel Pavlovich squatted down a short distance away and warmed himself by the fire, slicing almost transparent slivers from the half-eaten apple and blissfully popping them into his mouth.

In the tub where the neatly hacked chunks of wood were charring nicely, two weighty homemade soldering irons were heating away: iron rods with flat-irons welded to their ends. The coffin maker was stoking the seething fire with the iron that was not yet glowing, as he knowingly drew in the air with his rosy nose.

His thoughts, though, were not so much on the fire as on the drink that he was simultaneously preparing: hanging over the fire like a monkey was a sooty tin can holding on by its tail, its lid bent over the rim of the tub; inside it bubbled a tarry brew of thick narcotic-strength tea. It was beginning to steam, warming and delighting the craftsman's lively, tender eyes. 'There's nothing worse than being condemned as scrap, going to waste as good-for-nothing material. When the carpenter's found a use for you and the herbalist has too, then your time on earth keeps stretching on,' he said, as though singing the fire a lullaby.

'Sometimes I might pick up a rotten plank, and I'll be all wrapped up in myself. Then I'll think, "No, don't worry, I won't abandon you without finding some use for you. No matter how rotten you are, I'll get some woodchips out of you and boil up some *chifir* tea."'

'I like the smell of that smoke,' Pavel Pavlovich said to the craftsman. He swiped his jacket sleeve across lips that were sour perhaps from blood, perhaps from the apple he'd eaten, and held his calloused grey-blue hands to the fire. The sadness in his voice had a clean and simple *ting* to it, like glass.

'Smells good? Then be my guest. Let's down a gulp of this stuff to mellow out, we've time for a quick one.'

'No, no, I'm clean now. The old discipline was getting a bit lax, so I've tightened things up; now I just stick to dried-fruit drinks. What's that you were saying about planks? You reckon even rot can be of benefit if you put your heart into it? So where is that benefit? And who here has any heart? You're saying people will just roll over like those woodchips and let you reap benefit from them? Like hell. Every man, every living soul is like a splinter. We don't know how to forgive and let go, and even if we did, others wouldn't drop their grudges against us – it's just the way life is. Oh, the road is long! You can try to leave but you'll never escape. Then again, any time and any place you can come unstuck and drop from view. I wouldn't mind dropping from view myself . . . Turning up somewhere totally new. Ploughing the land? Or forging iron? Yeah, I can do all that. It's all the same to me: factory or farm, they need drivers everywhere, and I'm a top-notch driver. I'm just mad about the road. Ha! Now that's a lie, I couldn't enjoy it if I wanted to. Work is a beast. Everywhere is the same: you spend your time buggering off, chasing the four winds.' Then he spoke more softly, as though having a good grumble: 'Nobody likes me.'

'Who are you talking about?'

'I mean all those people banding together, when you're on your own in the world. People are a force. People can do whatever they want to you.'

'But why don't they like you?' the coffin maker asked in surprise.

'Because I don't like them, but I'm rubbish at pretending, and I don't want to apologise. And just for that, people won't let you live in peace,' he answered. 'But the thing is I don't like myself; every day I'm revolted by my own stench. I'll never learn to like it. And I'm revolted by fear. See, I always do the things that make me frightened. On principle. So that I can be stronger than my fear.'

They were approached by some guards: two unarmed soldiers who had been sent by the guard commander in his place. The tall Central Asian one could not understand that he was nobody's boss – perhaps with the exception of his small and grubby fellow guard, who respectfully kept his distance, enabling him both to be of service and to dodge any clips round the ear – and he looked about the place with a solemn expression. 'Eh, who are you?' For reasons known only to himself, he instantly decided to pick on Alyosha. 'Go, you go away . . . Understand, eh?'

Pavel Pavlovich bared his teeth. 'What you goggling at, you bastard? Can't recognise fellow soldiers when you see them?'

'What's up with you?' shouted the craftsman. 'So he's decided to act flash, but then the man's landed himself some power, how could he not gloat about it? Though it's not like one of life's big shots has turned up, is it? Take a look at him . . . When he was a wee nipper in his village I bet he never ate his fill and all he had to bring him joy was the blue sky above! So now he goes strutting about like a rooster . . . And let him, why not, he's not doing any harm! Well, no need to answer him back; we can make way, step aside for him – now where's the harm in that? You'd let a small kid go on ahead, you wouldn't take offence if he stamped his little foot. So show him pity like you would a child, if you're the one who's stronger. And if you're weaker, like I am, then give him some respect, ennoble him!'

Pavel Pavlovich took all this in and became cool-headed and stern. 'Nobody touches Alyosha when I'm around. The only person here who can tell me what to do is him,' he said as forcefully as though he could decree who would live and who would die.

By now the Central Asian guard was frightened and began making submissive gestures – he offered his hand in a brotherly way and mumbled something emotional. Changing the troubled tone of the conversation, the craftsman got back to the business at hand and brought up the subject of the missing head of the infirmary. His sighing over the fragrant tarry *chifir* tea, bubbling away with its promise of warmth and rest and gratuitous joy, gave way to a fear of being frozen to the spot. He flew into a flurry of ant-like activity, forcing the guards to take their places at the zinc trough and Alyosha and Pavel Pavlovich to fetch the body.

The woollen blanket that had hidden the unlovely cargo throughout the journey had been stripped away, crumpled up and shoved in a corner reeking of petrol.

They brought out the stretcher and in a flash they were back in the barn, having run nimbly as though it were raining and they were shivering with impatience to shelter. Everything they did felt effortless and liberating, their load did not weigh down their arms and the sight of it did not prey on their minds. As Alyosha hugged the body by the legs at the other end, he felt a surprising fluidity and airiness. Afterwards they all paused, realising that some kind of final and important moment had arrived for the stranger's dead body. 'Look how skinny he is, the clothes have gone all baggy on him,' the craftsman said with a sigh. Pavel Pavlovich grew quiet and wistful. 'I know they're a bit big, but they're new and only been worn twice,' said Kholmogorov, suddenly feeling guilty. The craftsman did not catch his drift. 'Yes, he's really withered. It means he was a good man. The good ones, see, they dry out and they might be dead but they don't give any stench, they just smell of straw.' He paused, noticing the plaster patch and realising it hid a fatal mark on the forehead. 'I see he's had more than his fair share of suffering. May God give his soul sanctuary. So that's how it is . . . Why did he have to go and do that, the poor dear? He must have lost all hope and faith.'

'Ah, but maybe he didn't put a bullet in his forehead all by himself? Maybe he was helped by someone higher ranking . . . Maybe it was even your God that did it! Or the guy might have been dead set against it – he was aiming for the sky but hit his forehead? I can smell a rat, oh what a rat . . . Huh, what am I saying! I can't just smell it – I know it. See, I know something that your God doesn't know, or that He's pretending not to know. I know it and I'm keeping my gob shut. Because each to his own. Every man for himself. Because that's how it has to be. But I'm not God. You know who is, though? The guy who pulled the trigger – he's God, because he has drawn the curtains on a life,' said Pavel Pavlovich.

'Now where's your boss got to? Forever hurrying, tells me to do the job within the hour, the next minute he's vanished in a puff of smoke,' said the coffin maker.

'He'll come running back when all the hard work's done; he's got a sixth sense for it – that's why he's the boss.'

'So it's farewell and God bless, then?'

'Too right it is. You've got a way with the bosses, like a wolf sussing out a sheep's hide, so why didn't you climb your way to the top? Too frightened, eh? Well then, Mukhin, so long! Afraid you lost in this life, sucker.'

'He's called Mukhin, as in "flies"? Then flies must run in the blood! The poor dear must have had family who flew around the place or buzzed about like pests. All of us living in God's bosom, we're flying around the place like flies, and the spot where the Grim Reaper wallops us becomes our heaven.'

'This one got walloped for sure. Caught in the wrong place at the wrong time.' Pavel Pavlovich stubbornly returned to his theme. 'Now we'll seal him in your crate and it will all be hushed up and buried.'

The old man hugged the coffin lid and laid it over the corpse decked out in dress uniform, ensconcing it in darkness.

Once the lid was in place, Pavel Pavlovich's face broke into a grin: on the side of the lid, stitched to the cloth and resembling a stamp, shone a yellow hammer and sickle. 'What times we live in, greybeard! I get it that the coffin is made of old fencing, but what's this symbol of the radiant future doing on its cover?'

'Didn't you know?' the coffin maker rounded on him heatedly. 'People gleefully stole all the fabric we had from the factory, but someone brought along two whole boxes of red flags from the club. The colour's gone and they're as tattered as rags; imagine how many years they spent flapping about in the wind on every holiday. So I didn't notice and ended up covering the coffin in a rag, and now this is showing . . . Oh, why did this have to happen? It's so embarrassing it makes you want to weep.'

'Come on, nail it down quick,' said Pavel Pavlovich. 'Citizen Boss has been trembling the whole journey, hanging his head, trying to carry out his orders . . . He's in a state, the old toothpuller.'

The head of the infirmary turned up when the zinc box was already partly sealed. He came running into the barn, scouring it as though searching for a mislaid cap. His hands were full: each held an unpleasant-looking puffy boiled sausage. 'You can eat now, boys,' the head of the infirmary said in a wavering voice, but the sombre face that he had prepared in advance did not harbour a shadow of doubt.

Bumping foreheads with the old man, Alyosha was pressing down the edge of the clean zinc sheet with a wooden block. Every so often a sigh of smoke would escape as the metal was tortured by the soldering iron. Pavel Pavlovich was also busy at work with the craftsman – he stood by, ready to bring in the soldering iron that was glowing away on the coals to replace the exhausted one. So the mention of food turned the air unpleasantly sour, as did the boiled sausages that Institutov was holding. It was only the two guards standing about idly, who must have been getting hungry as the day drew to an end, who shifted their gaze to the sausages that . Institutov was dangling more and more impatiently – until finally he tired of his burden and carefully placed the sausages on a clean and free corner of the now tranquil workbench that held the unfinished coffin.

All that could be heard in the barn was the gentle rumble of work. Institutov wandered along the finished products, casting a knowing eye over their senselessly yawning voids. His gaze naturally fell upon the feeble old man sitting on his stool in the corner of the barn. The head of the infirmary could not imagine that this man might just sit there in silence without any tangible purpose, and so he was careful to approach him generously: 'My dear man, why aren't you working along with everyone else?' The man who went by the name of Amadei Domianovich promptly announced from the corner: 'Disgusting.'

A change passed over Institutov's face. 'What can this mean, my dear man, may I ask?'

'Disgraceful,' the man echoed placidly in the corner.

'Now you're going too far, Comrade! Whatever do you mean?'

The answer rang out with a lusty finality: 'Lackey!'

The head of the infirmary called out hysterically: 'Guards, silence this prisoner!' The guards' eyes shot up from the workbench where the two unclaimed sausages were resting – but the two Central Asians sullenly failed to take in what had been said.

'He's my worker, we work as a pair . . . I do the coffins and he keeps an eye on the quality. It's always easier when there are two of you! Go and get some fresh air, Citizen Boss,' the coffin maker thoughtfully suggested.

With unnatural prudence, as though he were a circus horse taking a bow, Institutov butted his head against the empty air a few times and retreated backwards into the yard, but suddenly jumped and shrieked as though he were dying, pointing at the floor ahead of him where wood shavings were wriggling and hid something alive: 'Solder them in! Solder them in! Somebody do it!' Everyone froze, stunned by the screaming. But they did not find anything ghastly, or indeed anything new at all. Paler than a corpse, the head of the infirmary stood feebly, eyes bulging and mutely gulping like a fish with his gluttonous mouth. 'It's mice: he's scared to death of them,' Pavel Pavlovich said, grinning.

The work was done. The head of the infirmary hid in the ambulance unwilling to get out and fetch his order from the craftsman. Pavel Pavlovich backed the vehicle up to the shed entrance. One disgruntled glance from him was all it took to attract the assistance of the guards who were loafing about.

Just as they were about to grapple with the deathly load, the craftsman fell quiet and elicited silence. Then he turned to Pavel Pavlovich with an ingratiating look: 'Give us some parting words. Go on, my heart's longing to hear them.'

'Why bother with all that, greybeard? Let's get going.'

'Oh, you're all in such an eternal hurry . . . Amadei Domianovich! You say something at least. Dignify this death with your fine intellect.'

'Disgraceful!' cawed the mysteriously offended old man.

Then, disappointed, the coffin maker quietly intoned: 'Farewell, vast country, you unfortunate man.'

THE LONG FAREWELL

At Karaganda goods station, behind the solid wall around the railway warehouses, a funeral party of two – a clodhopping elderly warrant officer and a bashful young private – was awaiting its fate. Their meeting place was already submerged in twilight. They were as cold and hungry as prisoners of war. The jitters were teeming and biting them under the collar like lice. A sense of uncertainty brought together the ill-assorted strangers and from a distance, in the dark, they appeared like two stray dogs of some monstrous breed befriending one another: as tall as humans, tailless, with long grey pelts and duffle-bag bundles humped on their backs. The young soldier was still in service mode: poised in readiness and waiting at attention. Or perhaps for want of another superior, he was trying to be of service to the only senior present, listening to him as obediently as a son while the latter was busily scouring the area within two or three paces of them – spinning around, at times freezing to the spot as though he had heard a shout.

'Ivan Petrovich, tell me what Moscow's like.'

'Ah, they've got everything in Moscow, that's what it's like. You ever seen a banana? Nah, didn't think you had, but they've got them in Moscow. It's like they grow on trees there . . . How people live in the place I have no idea. See they've already got it all, there's no need to do anything, just keep picking up your wages and going on shopping sprees.'

'Ivan Petrovich, are we going to be there long?'

'We'll stay as long as we can; the funds allocated won't stretch that far. The funeral will take a day or two; they bury them awful quick. We'll be staying with the relatives – it was really lucky that I managed to sort that out. Would be good if they could feed us too, though I'm not sure they will. If our money and rations hold out, we could be there a week. We'll pluck up the courage and make out that we couldn't get hold of any train tickets back. We'll get it in the neck, of course, for each extra day – just so you're prepared!'

'But Ivan Petrovich, what will I be doing in Moscow?'

'Your job is easy enough: you just go wherever I go. And my job is straightforward too: not to do anything much, apart from carry out orders. Just be sure to keep your head, be quick but don't rush, otherwise things will get said later . . . They always come up with something to tick you off for. You'll be the whipping boy, and your whole life will be screwed up. You need to follow the middle path, then you'll be protected by the angels. Leave it to fools to do what they want, we'll do what we're told.'

The yawning moon appeared as a hazy luminous recess in the sky, gaping hungrily towards a number of tiny stars that were dangling like bait impaled on the points of fish hooks. But suddenly an impression of something belly-like arose in the night, as though everything had been swallowed up. All that remained near the buildings with their empty black windows, abandoned at this late hour, were some round desert islands of light, emerging from each of which was a stark tall palm of a lamp-post topped by a solitary glowing nut. Devoured in mist, the surroundings were constantly filling with animal sounds, with African roars and groans, as though ravening beasts were roaming, happy in their turn to gobble someone up. It was the nocturnal feast of the goods yard: eerily audible with its behemothic belly digesting all that was perpetually set in motion, powered by inhuman mechanisms under the command of human will. There was no hint of the station itself or its forecourt – there were only the prison walls of the left luggage office, the locked, deserted warehouses and the concrete carcasses of the locomotive sheds, reeking a fumy sweat of diesel.

The restless pair were illumined in the dark by distant headlights. The man and the young lad froze ignominiously against the wall, as if they had been mugged and stripped naked, and their two headless shadows reared and darted like cats in the gloom. A man dropped out of an ambulance as though springing from a cuckoo clock – and they recognised him: it was the head of the infirmary. He cried frantically: 'Comrades, time waits for no man! We'll show you the way! Follow me!' And he flew off. The vehicle pulled away, riding the bumps of the rocky wasteland. The soldiers jogged after it like a couple of tramps, until finally they had to break into a sprint.

At the concrete entrance ramp – an incline that was hardly steep but riddled with potholes – the clapped-out rattletrap ambulance faltered and the little men who were dutifully running after it shot ahead. Entirely hidden by a long tin awning, from which the huge sullen fortresses of identical storage sheds peered out as though scowling, the platform of the railway yard seemed distant and impenetrable. At the near end of the platform, some coupled wooden flour wagons were being loaded in complete silence: about ten taciturn labourers were carrying over sacks that coughed out dust on their shoulders. Burdened with the sacks, they remained just as reticent when parting to make way for the unusual procession; waiting sturdily, they watched as two panting soldiers ran from an austere coffin-like vehicle resembling a police van, while the correctional-olive-hued van drove on a few metres behind. 'They're chasing deserters,' the men said, sighing, and went back to work, their consciences clear.

Running ahead of the field ambulance, the warrant officer was chasing after the private. The procession flew past the next goods wagon being loaded alongside the platform. The young lad and the man following him were running so furiously in fear of getting mangled under the wheels that, when the vehicle stopped at its intended warehouse, they vanished at full pelt. For a long time the warrant officer heard shouts of 'To the top . . . To the top . . . ' from behind him, so he fled onwards, thinking they were racing to somewhere further on – while in fact, the head of the infirmary was yelling at the fleeing funeral team in vain: 'Stop! Stop!' The runners disappeared into the dark, and all that returned to Institutov was the echo of his own surprised yells. Two coupled wagons, a mail coach and a luggage van, were already standing at the platform. They looked as though they were taking a nap. The shunter that had hauled them over for loading exhaled the commotion of its labours, suffusing itself in fumy sweat – now it left for the next job; it was meant to return later to pull away with those same cars from the goods platform, in order to couple them to the long-haul passenger coaches and lead the train to its departure track.

'I mean really, this is outrageous . . . ' the head of the infirmary grumbled, feebly clapping his feet down on the resonant platform. 'Go after them and bring them back! Come on, quick!'

It was Kholmogorov who obeyed Institutov's order and took off down the platform. He disappeared so swiftly that Institutov shuddered, feeling engulfed by the almighty darkness. 'Look, you go. Quick, follow him.' He impatiently shoved Pavel Pavlovich into the gloom and when its black depths had swallowed the last person whom he might have bossed around, he was left utterly alone.

'I want to see my son,' the deserted Institutov suddenly heard from behind. He spun around in horror. The darkness expelled a small sullen figure with a briefcase and a hat, rather the way a man might officially turn up to collect his children from their mother's custody.

'What is it you want now? Have you been tailing me? Is this some sort of set-up? I'll call the police,' the head of the infirmary squeaked.

'My son Gennady might not be able to speak up, but he has me, his father. I've come to this town for the truth. I'm a nuclear engineer. I worked on the construction of the Obninsk nuclear power plant. I've done forty-five years of service. I took part in the emergency –'

'The Chernobyl disaster, haha!' Institutov livened up nervously, hoping only to muzzle the little man. 'Well, of course, these days we have every last tramp cleaning up some emergency or other. And I expect you, too, have suffered for the sake of humanity? You extinguished a nuclear fire? I can see you got well and truly irradiated; your coat and shirt have a nasty case of radiation sickness. Now, listen here. You are hideously drunk. No, my friend, you are mentally ill. Stop this blackmail at once and shove off or I'll put you in an asylum!'

The man in the hat's voice trembled, but he did not back down: 'Call the police. I demand to see my son's body!'

Institutov took a step back, but with an arrogant snicker. 'This is preposterous. This is unadulterated schizophrenia resulting from radiation poisoning, alcohol and, no doubt, your devastating paternal grief. I was ready to help you as the father. I offered to find you a hotel, provide you with a free ticket home. Look, I even shared your grief when you spent two days in a row barging into my office and maliciously obstructing me in the performance of my duties, but this – this is just too much! Please be so good as to explain whom and what you think we're hiding from you. The moment it happened, we straightaway telegraphed you the tragic news. Look, right here and now I am not entitled to hand you so much as the death certificate, but once the consignment arrives in that Moscow of yours, you'll get everything from our escorting soldiers, have no fear. What, we're hiding the body from you? Well it's hardly hidden if we ourselves are sending it to the funeral in the best possible shape! We don't have any incorruptible dead saints here, let alone refrigeration units for every corpse. A dead body in the medical sense is a perishable product. It has to travel all the way to its place of burial. You do realise we need to maintain basic hygiene, and a coffin involving zinc, you know, is not some sort of open house. What else do you have a problem with? Ah yes, you want us to dish up some guilty party . . . Just desperate for some kind of lurid sensationalism, right? Some action-packed detective story – with you starring in the lead role.'

'I want to know the truth about how my son died,' the uninvited father answered in a muffled voice.

'Only let's not have any crocodile tears – I have my own ideas of objectivity, see. You want to know the truth? You've thought it through? You're absolutely sure? Well, as you're in such moral torment, I'll break the rules. My friend, your son died by his own hand. How much deeper do you need to dig? No further if it's the truth you wanted to reach. That's right, now what are you gawping at? There you have it, your truth.'

Silence broke out. Institutov was meekly waiting for the moment he could go about comforting the finally devastated father. But the man crawled out from the wreckage and began groaning, unable to take any more pain: 'Gennady should have lived.'

'Well, you know, you should have told him that when he illegally acquired the guard commander's weapon, and no one knew whether his plans involved dying or killing.' Institutov wanted to prick this unfeeling noxious person with his words. 'You're an engineer, a nuclear scientist no less, and you're acting like a halfwit. You need to change your thinking, take a broader look, as a man of science. You want facts? You want food for thought? Your son died of his own free will. Now, by not raising a stink about it, we've ensured your right to material assistance and sympathy. But we're making all these funeral arrangements for your son, giving you the right to his pension, and you're insulting us! Yes, we deceived you, we wrote that he died in the line of duty, not out of pity for you, of course, but to keep our reputation clean. Well, there you have it. And we had reason to leave other facts out of the records too: we wanted to keep things amicable with you, none of this detective nonsense.

You want to find some guilty party – now don't go making a mistake, citizen, or you might stumble upon things best left untouched, like the fact that your son was the dregs of society. Will that make you feel any better?'

'I'm a nuclear engineer –'

'I know, I know . . . You think it's a hygienic matter to open up your darling son's coffin? To hell with your soul – let's just fight to the bitter end and gut the poor fellow, disembowel him? Rip him open! Find your facts! Eviscerate him! And then live with your precious truth until you yourself rot alive, in torment . . . So either you get permission from the Health Inspectorate for this vile unsanitary procedure or else make room for us to work. Get out, you nasty drunken idiot! Don't disgrace your son! Don't stain the last chapter of his biography, not that it could get much worse. Well I guess you'd better go and sire another one, before it's too late, a new one. Love him, pamper and mollycoddle him, name him Gennady too, build another nuclear power plant somewhere, perhaps it will all work out in the end. But right now things have not worked out – it means they were crossed by the stars. Don't you get it yet? It hasn't sunk in? You were just born unlucky, so what are you moaning about? What's this guilty party you're searching for? It's you, you're the one who's guilty, you drunken bastard. Guilty for being born, for living . . . It's you who drove your son to the grave the day you brought him into the world and started up your endless moaning . . . '

'Police!' A ghastly scream rang out in the dark. The little man in the hat blindly backed away, banged into the wall of the storage shed and slid down it in shock almost to the ground.

'Poli-i-ice!' the head of the infirmary suddenly sang out too. 'So where are they, your guardian police? They aren't here, my friend.' The small figure flattened himself against the wall and sagged, hanging there like a pretzel on a hook. 'Mukhin's father, pull yourself up straight, enough of your squatting!' Institutov said in disgust. 'As they say, the show is over. You can fly into a tantrum like this when you're with your drinking pals. Drunkenness doesn't do a man any favours. You should drink less. Keep off the bottle if you can't hold your drink. And your wife, Mukhin's mother, does she know about her son's death? I don't get it. She didn't come with you and, by the looks of it, you're a heavy drinker. Ah, could it be that she's a bit of a boozer too? Ha, so we should look for the pair of you in the gutter . . . But the thing is no one will bother. If it comes to it, we'll just bury him without you.'

Institutov had not allowed himself such blissful indulgence in a long time. He was saying all these words simply to inflict on the little man the most exquisite suffering possible. It was not even to make him hurt more and more, but rather to destroy him with this pain extracted from the man's very own mind and soul, as though zapping him with electric shocks. 'From now on I'll give them no pain relief whatsoever,' flashed through the toothpuller's mind.

The goods wagons were standing still, the warehouse was holding its peace, and the subordinates had gone astray. In this muddle, the medical officer knocked several times firmly on the warehouse gates, bawled at the luggage van and finally announced into the amorphous depths of the gloom, 'How long do I have to wait? This isn't the way to work. You need to show some conscience, Comrades; at the end of the day, you are our working class.'

In reply an unwashed head poked out from the vestibule of the luggage van: 'Oh, they've even turned up here, them bastard democrats . . . Go on, shout a bit louder, hold one of your protests! The moment the wagon appears, you're unhappy. Where's your patience, grumbling at everything. Got your own special conscience, have you? And it was all so fine, living and working was a joy. Why d'you have to come and muck everything up, you bugger? I feel sick with your type about. Go and slog your guts out yourself. Go on, you can kiss my arse . . . '

'Aargh!' shouted Institutov. 'Silence! Atten-shun! No, you'll work, you will. I'll teach you what work is . . . You'll be mining stone in the camps, you rotters, stacking up a mountain of your own crap!'

The luggage-van worker jumped as if scalded. He leaned his trunk out of the vestibule and began wailing like a woman: 'Now, why d'you have to be like that, boss, who's done any-thing to cross you? Anyone lifted a finger against you? Oh, you brute . . . Oh, good Lord . . . It's all going to the dogs. Call this a life, do you? I'm going, I'm on my way!'

A heart-rending iron shriek rang out from the wagon doors opening, as though some living creature were being ripped limb from limb. The guard started shouting bossily. Voices could be heard floating closer. A throng of freight handlers swept forward. In their midst a fat warehouse attendant was flapping about. There was a jangling of locks, and the warehouse released a sigh of greed. 'Ooh!' 'Hey,' 'Aah!' The workers' conversations were bubbling angrily, seething over in petty passions. As the luggage van was being loaded, the mail coach continued to stare emptily at the platform with its blind white-of-the-eye barred windows. Some people dressed in homely tracksuits came out to get a breath of air – they were government couriers – and with a soldierly uniformity they began proudly and dully strolling in pairs outside their coach, guarding their secrets.

Suddenly all the missing persons tumbled out of the dark onto the platform – and the workers stared sympathetically at the handful of wearied men in army uniform who were running past them again. 'Oooh,' Institutov gasped as if it were he who had been running. Then, stood there in his supervisor's pose, no longer bothering to goad anybody on, he sank into bliss once more. All bow-legged, the four men lugged the coffin, weighed it and filled out some forms, then packed it up, thus transforming the zinc sarcophagus into an ordinary freight package.

'Hello, Albert Gennadievich!' the warrant officer said in a guileless tone. He was happy that he'd drawn attention to himself, but then he went quiet, unsure what to add.

The small man, until this moment seemingly invisible, revived and came waltzing from the side towards the warrant officer. 'Mukhin's father, go back to your place!' boomed a sudden order. And the man in the hat stepped back listlessly. He complied.

The warrant officer was embarrassed and clearly had not realised that he was making a gaffe. Institutov drew close to him and hissed, looking him in the eye: 'What is the meaning of this, my friend?'

'Comrade Head of the Infirmary, honest, I don't even know myself what it means,' the warrant officer hastened to confess. 'Well, I think probably I got acquainted with Albert Gennadievich this morning, so it's not all that hard to understand. I guess that's what it means.'

'But what gave you the right to make his acquaintance? How did he get here in the first place? Wait – it was you, my friend, who set this up?' Institutov began to get worked up.

'Comrade Head of the Infirmary, I don't even understand it myself, I swear! We met only this morning when Albert Gennadievich – if I'm guilty then I apologise! – was standing there and I happened to be walking past with my private. Nobody could tell him when or where the cargo 200 would be shipped out, and he walked right up and asked me. I guess that's how he turned up here. But the fact that he's the father, I only found that out later. If I'd only known, you think I would have said a word? What, you think I don't know them regulations? It isn't my first time at this . . . '

'Oh shut up! Stop talking, you understand? Got it? Now, remember one thing, just one: from this moment you hold your tongue, button it. You keep away from him all the way to Moscow. If he latches on to you in the train, do not answer his questions. Keep your mouth shut: that is your number one mission.'

Upon hearing from the head of the infirmary what he must do to avoid getting into trouble, the warrant officer breathed a sigh of relief. 'Right. I'll keep silent, Comrade Head of the Infirmary. I'll button my mouth up tight, don't you worry,' he said zealously, shaking his head a few times with conviction, as though taking a vow of silence, and he almost fell quiet, but then he remembered something and, flapping and fussing as though laying up stores, began jabbering away, looking over Institutov's shoulder at somebody else: 'Albert Gennadievich, you know, as soon as my old woman heard about it, the old nag cornered me, she did! Buy a colour tv, she said, while you're in Moscow, and she wouldn't let up.

Do you think I'll be able to get one in your shops? I think I'd prefer a tv to a carpet. Well we can do without the carpet, we'd be better off with a tv. So we've agreed? A tv set? A colour one? Aw, thank you so much . . . It's not me – it's the wife. I would have liked a carpet, myself, or maybe something else. But the wife has set her heart on this tv of hers, and to hell with the cost! She says we can walk around the flat in slippers, it's not really a hardship, but you can only get a colour tv set in Moscow. Oh, look, excuse me, you've got this terrible grief, aw, you've lost your poor son, I'm so sorry . . . Uh, Comrade Head of the Infirmary. Uh, that's all, not another word.'

The warrant officer calmed down and suddenly went all limp, like a herring whose little skeleton had been whipped out. 'Mukhin's father, I see you're doing rather nicely,' Institutov turned his head, with a deathly boredom in his eyes. 'Fancy yourself a Chichikov, eh . . . Why not promise him a nice shiny car – a Volga, or a Lada at least. Do things Moscow style!'

They hauled the coffin-shaped crate – not the largest of boxes alongside the other packages, which held languishing cabinets, couches and other bulky human belongings – into a container and filled in the last gap in the luggage van. The entire farewell party and Institutov himself stood like heathen idols by the locked wagon. The couriers had long since vanished. The warehouse was already closed up.

A few freight handlers were still standing about to the side, shirking their duties. From somewhere in the dark their names were being hollered, but they did not go back. They were smoking. It looked as though they were taking aim with their *papirosa* cigarettes, killing time, and, like rifles after firing, the cigarettes were gently giving off smoke that smelt rancid, almost like the stench of gunpowder. Amid all this, one of them was calling attention to himself by mocking another of the men.

'Could you please keep it down; you're disturbing the peace!' Institutov said in their direction.

'This bloke loves his wife!' the laughing man responded, pointing out the other man, who meekly endured his mockery. 'Go on then, tell me why you love her. What's the meaning of it, this love for your wife?'

'Look, I didn't buy my love at the market, honestly! What do you mean, "Why"? I love her because she's a good person, because we've spent our whole lives together,' the man under interrogation forced out.

'And when she drops dead tomorrow, it's all gone. That's reality for you! And what will have been the point of your love for her?'

'But what about children? We've got a family, we're bringing up two kids. Ok, so we might die, but we'll be leaving them behind.'

'You do read what they write in the papers? Haven't you seen all those headlines? "Son stabs father to death". "Children dismember parents in bathroom". So what do you make of that then?'

'Just leave him alone! Why don't you give it a break, eh? Maybe you need a punch in the nose, clever clogs? If he believes he loves her, then why do you have to go poking about in his soul, not content until you've wrecked everything in it,' somebody said indignantly. 'Why is it you have to vandalise everything with your words? What do you gain from taking away someone's faith in love?'

'I'll share my answer with you all. You carry on building things with your faith in love, or in the pockmarked Devil or whatever, but build things properly, decently, so they can stand without crutches. But no, everything everywhere is coming to grief, because it's all held together with snot and spit. Of course, I could be kind and hold my tongue. You can always shut me up by brute force too. But if somebody's love for his wife doesn't stand up to my free speech, then that marriage is doomed. It's a self-evident truth. Brawls, alcoholism and poverty – that's love for you.'

These questions asked without the least desire to find anything out certainly flummoxed all the hapless listeners. Having sown dejection and shame among his workmates, the sharp-witted worker now sounded off with a pompous smirk amid all these fools: 'Marry, reproduce . . . First you slog away for your wives and children, then for your medicines – and then for your coffin. You can go grovelling to your wives for your own hard-earned cash whenever you fancy a beer. Spend twenty years busting a gut for your children, only for them to run off to the register office – and bam, they're gone, and they were ashamed to invite the likes of you to the wedding. Every day of your life is the same: you munch your macaroni, haul your hernia around and have a good moan about life not giving you enough. As for me, I'm going to make my life a party. I'm not going to devote my life to doing my duties. It will all be just for me. All the women I want, I'll buy myself a suit, hang out in restaurants – and I'll toil away here with you guys putting aside the same again for my old age. And if some little cherub should come into the world then he can jolly well thank me and give me a bow for creating him for free.'

Everyone stamped out their cigarettes and went off, heavy-hearted, back to their work. The worker strode in the same direction, rather pleased with himself. The platform had emptied. A quiver of expectation rippled through the air as at the moment before a train departs. The two coupled wagons, though, just stood there like lone tree stumps.

'As I see it, the time has come to say farewell,' said Institutov, but something about his own words was involuntarily weighing upon him. 'In a few days' time, this wagon will arrive in Gennady's home town, unless, of course, the train is derailed. Reality isn't pampering us with good news any more. Everything is getting blasted to pieces, burning in flames and sinking like a rock. Gennady's life, too, was woefully brief. It was broken off tragically, in mid-flight, but let's not talk about such depressing stuff. Better to remember Gennady once more. We'll think of him and send him on his final journey with a minute's silence. Gennady, I'm sorry we couldn't protect you. Goodbye, my friend.'

That should have been the end of it. But the expectation of that end drew on and on. Institutov stood there uncomfortably for well over a minute, then, suddenly ashamed of this moment of tenderness, he rather clownishly could not resist enlivening the lament with a joke of his own. 'The railway is the most reliable means of transport there is. Perhaps that can't be said for the rest of us, but the rails and sleepers are here to stay! Right, let's get down to the station. Our warrant officer can check that the precious cargo is still in order – and then it's off to the capital. Colour television, eh? I wouldn't mind making such a rare purchase for our times myself. By the way, Mukhin's father, you'll be coming with us. See, there'll be less worry that way. We don't want the train leaving without you. Warrant Officer, you don't happen to have tickets for the same coach as Mukhin's father? Well in any case, we'll find out soon enough . . . To the station, my friends!'

But Mukhin's father started muttering tearfully, 'Today is the ninth day since Gennady was taken from us. Comrades, may I ask you to join me in my hotel to mark the occasion?'

'Shame on you, cashing in on the memory of your own son!' Institutov burst out in rage. 'His death happened six days ago. You can have your booze-up when you get to Moscow. Or maybe you want to rustle up some birthday or other? How can you have a remembrance drink if he's not yet in the ground? No, it's simply a case of the DTs. Grab this mental case and haul him into the ambulance, no need to mollycoddle the wino.' But no one dared drag the little man anywhere. 'What's this? Have all of you taken leave of your senses? Oh some father he is! He treats his own son's death as an excuse to pour himself another drink, and there you have it. No, my friend, be patient, you can pickle yourself stupid on the train, but right now we're short of time.'

'Comrades, may I ask you to mark the occasion with me,' Mukhin's father reiterated plaintively. 'I'd like to invite you all back to my hotel; it isn't far. We have plenty of time before the train departs. No need to fret, you'll make it in time.'

'And you, my friend, aren't you in a hurry yourself? No, I'm sorry, it's out of the question! Wait a minute, hotel? What hotel? Your train leaves in an hour . . . Now, listen, show me your ticket. You do have a ticket, don't you? Answer me, Mukhin's father, you didn't drink your ticket money away did you? You nasty little man, don't you think you ought to show up at your own son's funeral?'

The inebriated man cast down his eyes and intoned under his breath: 'Comrades . . . Gennady and I invite you. There isn't a nation in the world that wouldn't mark the occasion . . . '

'Look, why do you keep fibbing to everyone?' shouted Institutov.

But the dejected little man fell silent. The warrant officer, until now diligently keeping quiet as ordered, now bolted nervously over to the head of the infirmary and whined, 'Albert Gennadievich has no ticket, you say? How will he get on the train without a ticket?'

'Look, can you please keep out of this! What's it got to do with you? Fancy yourself an Uncle Vanya, eh . . . '

The simple-hearted warrant officer drew himself up, as though thrusting his chest against a wall, and, all of a sudden tearing up, he rebelled: 'What it has to do with me, Comrade Head of the Infirmary, is that he promised we could stay at his apartment. All you can say is "silence, silence", well you're the one, pardon me, who's playing the fool! I wasn't expecting to have to sleep in the station. So it's Moscow, and what of it! The instant your train pulls in, they fleece you for all you got. Me and my private will be getting just thirty kopecks each per day, and you tell me to shut up. You can't even eat decently on that, not even a dog's dinner. He promised me, he said: "Ivan Petrovich, you can stay at my place, no charge." What'll I tell the wife: that I've blown all the money on a hotel? And what about the telly, the carpet? All our lives we've been frugal, scrimping and saving . . . '

Mukhin's father spoke up in a mournful voice: 'Ivan, I invite you –'

'Don't even think of asking – what a nasty let-down, Albert. I trusted you like you was family. I believed you, but now you've tricked me you're a complete stranger to me, I'll have you know. Comrade Head of the Infirmary, I'll only trust you from now on. Maybe you can shove the bugger on the train, eh? And he's lying, even about the hotel; I saw it, and it wasn't a hotel room, it was a rail coach on wheels. Come on, let's force him into the train. Let's make him go, let's make him bury his son, the damn alimony dodger.'

'Absolutely not – end of story. Let him stay here. Now if there's one person I'm not sorry for . . . ' Institutov said.

'But wait, boss. I'm going to accept the invitation. I'm crazy about old traditions.' Institutov span around, as though to grab at something in the air, and it was only this that saved him from falling. He feebly scanned their faces, still believing he had imagined this voice. 'Let's go, Dad. Where did you plan on heading? Don't you fear: we'll mark his memory in proper style.' Pavel Pavlovich went over to the small man and stood by his side, placing his hand on the man's shoulder. Mukhin's father raised his head, then smiled vacantly through his tears and said, 'Nuclear workers, forward march!' At that very moment his hat fell from his head. The little man looked down indifferently at the headwear that had fallen at his feet, and Pavel Pavlovich got upset: 'Well, pick up your hat.' But Institutov ran and grabbed the hat in a trice, and, clearly not intending to return it, he wailed: 'Where are we off to? Who's going? Why are they going?'

'Give back the hat! It's not yours!' barked Pavel Pavlovich.

'I won't give it back! I won't!' said Institutov loudly.

'Do you need your hat, Dad? Well, do you?'

'I don't need the hat,' the man replied in a limp and listless voice. Pavel Pavlovich slackened, shivered, and something shot through him like lightning.

'My friend, you are heading straight for the prison camp – what do you think you're doing?' Institutov bleated piteously. 'No, wait, stop! I agree, I agree! We'll go to the station and then we can go wherever you want; I accept the invitation too! Stop, you're forgetting we have the ambulance. I order you to stop. Where are you going? Think about what you're doing, you're signing your own death sentence . . . And you'll rot behind bars . . . And as for you, you're sticking your head in a noose . . . '

The last person whose fate was foretold by the head of the infirmary, though no longer with any hope of calling him back, was Alyosha Kholmogorov. He was running clumsily along the platform, trying to catch up with the men who were slowly disappearing into the pitch-dark distance. Institutov suddenly thought of something as he registered the running figure and, whether in joy or envy, he called after him, 'And you'll never see your teeth!' The two servicemen assigned to the funeral team shuddered. 'Comrade Head of the Infirmary, everybody is running – what about us?' the simple-hearted warrant officer pleaded all in a fluster, ready, if need be, to run too.

ON THE ROAD

While they were still on the platform loading the coffin, Kholmogorov had recognised the intruder as the citizen who had
turned up that morning at the infirmary. He hadn't known
him by his face but by his hat, when the drunken man had
slumped against the wall, dropping his head to his chest,
his face hidden to the chin behind the hat's wide-brimmed
halo. Alyosha was afraid that the drunken man might raise
his head, glance at him and recognise him too. At one point
he had indeed stopped, turned around and asked in surprise:
'Who are you? Are you Gennady's comrades? There isn't
enough room for you all . . . ' But then he had lowered his
head and strode on.

Mukhin's father was leading them away irrevocably into
the depths of this terrain, which in shape and content resembled a cemetery and ran along the endless bony roads of the
train tracks. The remains of rails and sleepers kept showing
up underfoot, overgrown with grass or almost levelled to
the ground.

The hum of express trains sounded unearthly, as if from
some distant world. Pavel Pavlovich had travelled the length
and breadth of Karaganda but he could not remember any
hotels in this vicinity. The station stood by itself on the edge

of town, at the spot where the streets filled with high-rise apartment blocks ended and wooden houses began swarming like hives. The thought flashed through Pavel Pavlovich's mind that the drunken little guy no longer knew where he was going. But he could not muster the courage to stop and interrogate the man leading them into the unknown. 'Maybe I should snuff someone out,' he said suddenly through his teeth, as though nothing were amiss, then he called out loudly over his shoulder, 'Hey, skin-and-bones, have you really been demobbed, or were you just saying it to act flash?'

'No, it's true. Tomorrow I'm catching the train and going home,' Kholmogorov rushed to say but he faltered on the last word. The two runaways nursed their own silence.

Signal lights suddenly glimmered across the mute expanse, whither the railroad track flowed like a river of paths before scattering to the four winds in a hundred directions. Mukhin's father swung down from the embankment and found himself on the tracks, stepping across the rails in sweeping strokes like a swimmer. No sooner had he entered the territory of the fathomless steel lines than a commuter train swept ruthlessly along a set of them, slashing the darkness with its blade of light. It passed some way off, but as though it were rushing to kill somebody. While they were crossing the rail tracks, which were almost invisible in the gloom, it seemed as though two tiny balls of lightning were rolling down from a height. Their racing light was expanding inexorably and all around the rails were sparking like fuses. The entire expanse was streaked with rectilinear lightning, each bolt tracing its own path; these, too, were racing along underfoot. Feeling queasy and frightened, Pavel Pavlovich grabbed Alyosha and dragged him onto a narrow island. The little man was calmly pacing along a blade of steel lightning. 'Stop! You'll get killed! There's a train coming! Get down!' a bloodcurdling shout rang out. Mukhin's father halted, he even turned around – but the rushing roar and light dazed him, rooting him to the spot.

As the small figure on the tracks froze, a rattlesnake freight train revealed itself and a moment later stretched out in its final pounce. They saw with their own eyes how the straight rails carrying the freight train were squeezing the man in a vice. His entire figure, standing a hundred odd metres from the train, became blacker than a shadow. The electric locomotive did not lose speed. The man did not climb off the track. But when the roaring, lights and whirlwind suddenly whooshed past, and a thundering, hurtling wall of wagons flowed in their turn behind his pathetic little figure, it became patently clear that the drunk had not consciously intended to fall under a train. The swirl of the speeding train had either horrified or deafened him. He clutched his head in his hands, then withdrew his hands and stretched them out as though fumbling for something nearby – moving closer and closer to the ground until he was kneeling. On the ground he continued to grope, agonising and crawling back and forth. His longish greying hair, a steely mother-of-pearl hue, tousled by the whizzing train, seemed to give his head wings, making it look like a mighty bird. But when the last wagon had flown by, his head flopped and his hair hung weeping and sad, leaving his face barely peeping out.

'My hat's gone . . . Where's my hat?' Mukhin's father lamented as they lifted him from his knees.

Pavel Pavlovich said angrily, 'Oh, who cares about the hat! You're a ruddy hat yourself.'

'Where's my hat gone?' the little man objected.

'Forget about the hat. Quick, let's go!' barked Pavel Pavlovich.

'Give me my hat back! Oh, why are you doing this to me, lads?' Mukhin's father implored.

'Look, Dad, we don't have your hat, can't you understand? It's gone wherever the train blew it.'

'Ah, it's blown away . . . ' He calmed down.

'Here, have your suitcase. That didn't get blown away.'

'Thank you,' Mukhin's father said, and the heavy briefcase was hung from the arm of its owner. 'Lads, may I ask you, on this occasion, to enter the reactor hall. It is nine days today since my son Gennady departed. I ask you all to commemorate the date with me. You understand people have expressed willingness to come out of their deep respect for me.'

'We do, we understand,' Pavel Pavlovich said with a grin, and he whispered furtively to Alyosha: 'Looks like we've hit the end of the line. Well, what do you think? Maybe you should head back. Tomorrow you can buzz off to your freedom – so do it. You still gotta get some clobber from the doctor, give yourself a wash, comb your hair, while me and Dad can wander off wherever. Me and Dad have nowhere to hurry to any more.'

Kholmogorov whispered back, believing that he too was confiding something special to Pavel Pavlovich: 'It's ok, I've got plenty of time. But you left the ambulance back at the station . . . Maybe you better go back? Otherwise how will they get to the station without you?'

'Won't take them long to walk it. The main thing is the luggage has been handed in, they're off the hook,' said Pavel Pavlovich. 'Now for *us* to make our escape . . . Maybe we could make a run for Moscow ourselves? Moscow's big, there's room enough for everyone.'

'This hotel seems a long way away. Do you think he's lost his way? What's going to happen now? If all the guests are there already, they'll think he's gone back home or something, and they'll all leave.'

'Don't fall behind, lads, people are waiting for us!' Mukhin's father piped up.

'Don't fall behind! There are people, people!' Pavel Pavlovich called out, shaking with laughter. 'People, I'm on my way to you! Oh, how I adore people!'

Oblivious to everything and everyone, he was driven on by his own insolent cackling laughter. Suddenly he stumbled on the rails. He fell. He went quiet; he got up. And he became ferociously lonely. With a muffled growl, he kicked the rails before crossing them. Once they'd received a bashing from his boots, they slipped from his attention. He vacantly threaded his way over the meridians of steel corpses with their narrow worm-like bodies. The lights of a train flashed. And now it was Pavel Pavlovich who remained standing right on the tracks, spewing swear words and curses. A passenger train whizzed past him. 'Oh piss off, you dirty bastard, you son of a bitch!' he yelled in anguish with all his might, seeing in the chain of carriages racing past a palpably hateful chariot of death.

He had believed this restless journey along the rails could only have one purpose: to cross the tracks. But the little man was leading his sluggish companions further and further in the same direction as the trains.

It was becoming inexplicably quieter and darker. The noise and lights were drifting into the distance. Issuing from the night like lost souls were individual carriages and entire trains, standing motionless on the tracks, severed from their fiery, racing electric heads, as though they had been slain by somebody one jump ahead. There was not a sign or sound suggesting human presence. Mukhin's father fearlessly entered the labyrinth of carriages. Having quietened down, Pavel Pavlovich looked about like a child amid the discarded, seemingly giant rail carriages, which harboured no life inside, no doubt thinking he had awoken in his own personal hell. Identical round-cornered windows glinted with darkness, as though he were peering into a well. Suddenly popping into view, set here and there in the windows, were white plates with carriage numbers – 2, 12, 6, 9, 3, 10, 8. The numbers resembled those found on tear-off calendars and were as surprising to find there as faces, inspiring dread each time they appeared.

The two trains they passed on their narrow, well-trodden path also had placards reminiscent of the street signs found in any suburb. It was as if each carriage were a house in its own street.

Little bluish houses stretched on down one side, with signs that read 'TSELINOGRAD–NOVOKUZNETSK'. On one placard the letters were squashed up with sadness, while another had been effaced by time, then with a sudden jolt of realism there would be a spanking new one, lively and conscious, on which the letters would not even allow themselves to be read, as though it meant being stripped naked. On their other side stood a sombre bog-coloured train, the Turkestan: its single-humped roofs were the carriages, coupled together like camels in a caravan. And beyond them were some raddled ones, no better than minecarts, with the nameplate 'KUSHKA–VORKUTA'.

No sooner had they passed a train than the next began. At one point Mukhin's father turned off into a gap between them, but there was no end to the carriages. They stood like walls, scattered all over in a giddying labyrinth. The trains stretched on, one after the other, giving the impression almost of genuine towns – too numerous to count or remember.

It might have been an apparition seen by desperate men were it not a reality: on the tracks, peaceful, lively lights were shining, and there was the smell of wood smoke from stoves. Tucked away in a dead end, and thus lending the scene a typically rustic feel, a train stood on the rails, overgrown with ancient life, like a tree stump. From the russet-coloured carriages' tin chimneys, whitish smoke was ascending in earnest into the night sky, and from the simple wooden steps put up to provide entrances to the vestibules, warm tarry light spilled onto the ground. Opposite each carriage lay a mound of anthracite and a puddle shimmering like anthracite in the moonlight; washing hung just like in a backyard, even if the line did stretch from carriage to carriage: underwear, sheets, trousers, dresses and shirts. Almost every window, with drapes tied back in the manner of stage curtains, seemed like a puppet theatre – one where bottles, vases and glasses were acting out joy and sadness as though they were alive. Along the entire length of the train, daubed in white paint, were the words HOTEL, HOTEL, HOTEL, HOTEL. A dog was barking somewhere. A baby could be heard crying; there was the smell of cooking.

A housewifely woman with a bucket came out onto one set of steps and tossed her dirty water into the darkness. She glanced at the people walking through the yard and said in a singsong, 'Ooh, hello there, Albert Gennadievich, I hope I didn't splash you or your guests.'

'Not at all, Galya, my dear. Earthly dirt doesn't affect atomic scientists. I have everything under control. Background radiation levels are within the normal range,' reported Mukhin's father loudly.

'Oh, Albert Gennadievich, what's happened to the hat you were wearing?'

'There was an emergency, my darling, but we'll talk about it in private. You're always hard at work, pottering away. Doing the family washing are you?'

'Family washing, not likely – it's for them refugees: they're spreading their filth everywhere. Just like gypsies, I tell you. They don't work, get everything dirty and they're rude to you. Go around killing each other, burning and ransacking everything at home, and then they turn up here with their grime. We could be catching lice from them soon. And the authorities in their wisdom just had to put refugees in the same hotel as passengers! We have to cough up for our compartment, but they get theirs for free – just because they're refugees, should we all be made to suffer?'

Tormented by her voluptuous hankering body, the woman was not so much objecting or complaining as flaunting herself. She knitted her brows, threw her arms up in the air, swivelled as if she were on a pedestal, inviting glances from all angles. But Mukhin's father had already turned gloomy and he eagerly put her wise as to what was happening: 'The country is undergoing thermonuclear disintegration. According to my forecasts, it will take fifteen years for the situation to change. Not all of us will live that long, but I have faith in atomic energy. We have enough uranium reserves. We'll have light and warmth, and that's the important thing. Nuclear workers will never let you down.'

'Oh, Albert Gennadievich, you make it all so easy to understand. It immediately seems so logical: such logic for the heart! Thank you, I'm much calmer after that; had rats gnawing at my heart before. Oh, I keep nattering on about my own stuff, but you were taken to the site of your son's heroic deed today.'

'With two generals in a black Volga. These are Gennady's comrades-in-arms accompanying me. I'm not at liberty to say any more. I signed a non-disclosure agreement. The circumstances of my son's death will only be declassified in forty-three years' time.'

'Ooh, what an important mission he must have performed, seeing as it's all so hush-hush. Maybe they'll give him a posthumous award, Albert Gennadievich, maybe even a Hero medal! Oh, of course you can't get your son back, well that's life for you. The heroes have to die, they don't even get to live a little bit.'

'The coffin's being sent by train to Moscow. And I, my dear nuclear scientists, will be catching a plane in the next few days. Today it's nine days since Gennady passed away. Galya, love, I'd like you to mark this occasion with me. I've invited only trusted and reliable persons. May I ask you to enter the reactor hall . . . '

'Yes, yes, I know . . . I'm coming. I'll bring my pancakes, eh, Albert Gennadievich!' she said in a singsong.

'Lads, I'm ready.' Mukhin's father turned glumly to the young men in uniform, as though he were under their protection. But when they left, he said matter-of-factly and with a certain lusty admiration: 'What a woman – a real Arabian steed! She's the wife of a colonel in the Space Forces. Her husband's serving in Baikonur, a personal friend of Yuri Gagarin. She was fearlessly unfaithful to him in her search for true love. He threw her out with the two kids. She's on her way to her mother in Ulyanovsk, just waiting for the tickets. Size four bust. Buys her flour on the black market. Her pancakes with egg and cabbage are out of this orbit. They make a first-rate *hors d'oeuvre*.'

The drunken man had come to life – he had even sobered up a bit, perhaps at the prospect of some booze. Fatigue had not seriously hit him during the entire walk there. 'May I ask you to go straight into the reactor hall,' he said for the umpteenth time with extravagant generosity, inviting them up the steps of one of the russet carriages. The huge metal door with its porthole, which opened onto the vestibule, was locked. But no sooner had Mukhin's father banged on it boldly with his fist than a clear and simple face greeted them from the other side.

'Reporting to Albertych: all persons are assembled and the table was spread ages ago! We were worried about you. Some of us even thought you weren't coming. But I knew you'd be back, you'd keep your word,' the deft man said admiringly. It seemed in his dosshouse-on-wheels he was still working as a conductor and had even dressed for the evening in full uniform: a peaked cap with railway insignia, a suit, shirt and tie.

'Who are the people? Are they trusted? Reliable?' the little man asked anxiously.

'They're trusted and reliable. The table is laid, everybody's assembled and waiting. Albertych, don't you worry,' said the man in the dark blue transport-ministry uniform.

'Do you realise what date it is today? We need to get the reactor operating at full capacity. Today, nuclear engineer Albert Mukhin is paying his last respects to his son.'

The conductor replied solemnly and sincerely 'I am fully aware of it. We're sending him off to God in Heaven, we'll do everything properly, Albertych, don't you worry.'

'All right, you've got it,' mumbled Mukhin's father, growing listless again. 'These two are with me. And no questions.'

'Come on, then, why are you standing out in the cold! Here, let me take your briefcase. Young men, be our guests, we'll be brothers. We'll all be one, don't you worry. Albertych! Where's your hat? What happened?'

'It's gone, old chap. End of story. Let's forget about it. Life is shit, old chap, everything in this life is total shit. Everything! With the exception of nuclear energy, friendship . . . and death.'

The carriage turned out to be a third-class one, of the kind in which thousands upon thousands were journeying at that very moment, travelling across all the territories, regions, republics and cities throughout the vast country. The ceiling seemed to be leaking electric light. It was cramped in the gangway. A fog of comestible odours hung in the air from the fried and the boiled, the home-cooked, the shop-bought and the rations, all mingling together and gently decomposing in the living warmth. There were bashful screen partitions. The berths to the left and right were all vacant, without a soul, but the sound of voices was growing ever more distinct. Mukhin's father walked towards the din with such pomposity that he forced the others to pile up behind him. 'Amazing man, one of a kind.' The irrepressible conductor of the third-class carriage was already pushing them from the back.

'Not like us! We just live and sleep, but a man like that lives
for us all without sleeping a wink. Any other bloke would
have got a job in trade or something, just for himself, but
this man picked a profession that brings warmth and light
to everybody. Always busy worrying his head and explain-
ing things, presenting ideas and inventing stuff. And think
of what he suffers! Wherever there's a catastrophe in the
country – there he is, saving the day! He's given all he's got,
even his son. And we're not taking proper care of the man,
'cause we're too busy looking after ourselves.'

They came upon people in the second half of the carriage.
The bay where they had gathered must have been where
Mukhin's father was lodging; he spoke of his own bunk there
as his 'room'. They welcomed him with a mournful silence that
seemed as though everyone had pooled together to purchase
it. About a dozen guests were sitting at a table spread with
what was clearly a funeral feast. The table had been impro-
vised. Some resourceful soul had bridged the folding tables
by the windows at opposite sides of the carriage with a plank.
The homemade table-top was covered in white sheets. The
resulting arrangement made for a convincing funeral altar;
its entire length could have accommodated the coffin of the
person they were seeing off. The guests were squashed up
along it on the passenger seats: they had occupied the lower
berths, and people were also sitting in the aisles on boards
spanning the gaps like little bridges. On the upper bunks –
even on the perpendicular one in the gangway – there lay
three more guests, whose heads hung silently over the feast
like globe lampshades.

Upon the host's arrival, one of the bottom bunks was
immediately vacated and offered to the nuclear engineer.

Behaving as though the young men in uniform were his guards, he maintained a morose and lofty silence. All this had a dramatic effect on the people gathered. The guests froze in their places, gazing at Mukhin's father with a similarly sullen grandeur, while he surveyed the offerings with the pride and indifference of a well-fed man. His stern gaze sought alcohol and could be tempted only by bottled refreshments. His eyes settled firmly on the neck of a bottle, whose contents seemed not to be moonshine, and glazed over. 'We have vodka?' he marvelled involuntarily, entranced. 'Don't you worry, Albertych, the very stuff, purchased with ration coupons, especially for you. And also some cans and sunflower oil from the humanitarian aid. I offered up my whole supply.' The conductor brought this up casually in front of the guests, though he also reddened bashfully.

'Then may I ask you to pour me one-fifty mils,' Mukhin's father said promptly. 'Fill everybody's glasses! I declare all systems go. Could I ask you all to pay attention?'

His demeanour fell somewhere between odious and pathetic during this moment of liveliness, yet his audience were listening carefully and were all set for mourning. But, when he began speaking about himself, grief swept over his face too; it was as if he had turned up at his own funeral. 'The universe is made up of atoms, and I, Albert Mukhin, was involved with an association in this country known as Spetsatom. A universe without atoms would be a shitty place. One hour ago, I was standing by my son's coffin, and I did not feel ashamed of him. Albert Mukhin's son has become an atom in the universe. He departed like a real nuclear scientist, walking into his own blazing reactor . . . May I ask each and every one of you to appreciate that? And now I'll say, in the words of my favourite poet, Yevgeny Yevtushenko: *Death is no harbour – Death breaks the journey of the ship!* Gennady, your father is with you. I forgive you for what you did, old chap. We'll meet in the universe!'

After the speech, Mukhin's father refuelled with another 150ml of vodka and lost all interest in the goings-on. Of necessity, people were still hovering with their food. He did not chase his drink with a bite of anything; instead he fixed his gaze on the empty tumbler, which made the commotion at the table suddenly seem disconnected, indecorous, even. The guests quietened down prematurely – yet he continued to dwell in complete silence in front of the glass, as though it contained all his grief. Unable to bear the silence a moment longer and, no doubt, meaning well, somebody piped up with a heartfelt question: 'But tell us, what was it that caused Gennady's death?'

'My son died defending democracy,' said Mukhin's father, hammering out the words. The third-class carriage soared upward in a kind of weary descent. There were no more questions. Nobody ventured to query this or even enquire further, let alone hint at an alternative. They all waited nobly for the minute of silence to end, but again someone was barely able to endure it and rose to their full height, bursting with lofty emotions like a convict during sentencing, but Mukhin's father stubbornly refused to unseal his lips, and so for almost every person the silence turned into torture by shame.

'Albertych, what's wrong?' The conductor felt frightened.

'My son wasn't poured any vodka,' he said, his face unaltered.

'What's this? You think somebody is being stingy with the vodka? Honestly!'

A commotion broke out: they rustled up a glass, poured some vodka and placed a slice of black bread on top. Mukhin's father said, 'Put my glass next to Gennady's.' When the conductor had silently carried out his wishes, Mukhin's father suddenly shocked people with the command, 'Everybody drink!' The guests downed their glasses in one, but then they noticed that he had not touched his.

'Albertovich! What's all this about?'

'I won't be drinking any more today. That's just the way it is, old chap. People – may I ask you all to remain where you are.'

The reassured guests stayed in their seats and began hurriedly eating the snacks. The herring and meat in aspic were soon gone, and they filled up by munching on bread and packing in potatoes. The bulk of the food was quickly consumed. Then began the conversations about life and death. The guests on the top berths piped up first, as they needed assistance to receive their nibbles. And it was they who began philosophising with those sitting below, who were glumly handing them plates.

One muttonish dame dressed as lamb, who was quickly becoming inebriated, grew bolder and began serving the two soldiers in the manner of a hostess. She heaped up two plates with inedible watery pudding, then cried out with petulant languor and sweetness: 'Why aren't you drinking, men?'

Pavel Pavlovich, upon whom the lady was lavishing a gaze bubbling with puzzlement, grinned at her and replied impetuously, 'A real man is the last to drink and the first to sober up.'

'So, mister, you're a real man are you? Ooh, I don't think I introduced myself! I'm Yelena. And you are . . . ?'

'To friends and whores I'm simply Rafael.' The lady shrank back into loneliness. Patches of mauve showed through the rough coating of face powder tinted with girlish blusher.

Deciding not to take offence too quickly, she spoke in the haughty, nonchalant tone of a teacher: 'I'm sorry, but which category of acquaintance do you put me in?'

Pavel Pavlovich paused, forcing the lady to wait, then suddenly he smiled: 'Ah but we aren't acquainted; I haven't drunk vodka with you yet.'

'Well then let us perform that rite,' the tipsy lady replied giddily.

'Helen of Troy,' he whispered so that only she could hear it.

'Rafael, let's be friends. Let's drink, Rafael.' Her babbling fluttered over the feast.

'You bet, and with such a luscious woman!' said the real man, and his eyes shone with a cruel, macabre spark.

The lady tried to endow her clumsy inebriated tottering around the table with a kind of elaborate elegance. She was waltzing around the glasses of vodka that had been left side by side for father and son and that everybody else was ignoring, happy drinking their moonshine. She wanted to pinch them on the sly, but Mukhin's father was hindering her, his vacant mournful gaze also roving around this tumbler monument, erected on the table at his behest. 'Why's nobody drinking that vodka? Someone's got to drink it so it won't go to waste,' she said finally.

'That ration is sacred. The ration for the dead man and the living one: once poured, it's always forgotten. You see, Yelena, baby, everything here is deeply soulful, though it might look from the outside like an ordinary still life. The glass is the grave. They cover it with black bread – it's like sprinkling earth on the grave. The vodka in the glass, that's the soul. When it evaporates and the glass is empty – that's it, the ordeal is over, the soul is gone. And right now we're sitting here like fools, observing this natural phenomenon.'

'Haha, Rafael, what a funny joke! I don't want to know about these horrors of yours. I hate them! Sorry, but I'm still alive. I want to know all about flowers, and the sea, and love . . . '

This sounded like blasphemy. Being respectable people, the nearest guests turned their backs on the lady. And little by little they all began arguing over each other about love and death – noisily, rowdily, their tongues flickering like flames. Everybody was puffing out their chests, almost bobbing up and down, making sure their presence was felt and their opinions vented. Demented shouts were continually ringing out over the hubbub: 'Love is sex;' 'There is no God.' And whenever he emerged from his reverie, each time disagreeing with everything and everyone, Mukhin's father would boom in farewell: 'I'll wipe e-v-e-r-y-thing out!'

The arguers were burning away like firewood. Soon the bonfire subsided into a mournful flickering, and the debaters broke up into clusters. Dismayed, some people stopped speaking entirely.

Beyond the windows of the carriages the night was inkblack. For a while nothing particularly significant occurred – except, perhaps, for the brief appearance of the pancakes the woman had promised Mukhin's father. She remained at his side, angry at everybody for gobbling up her offering. People from the other carriages began wandering towards the noise. They hung around in the narrow gangway as though queueing, no doubt from force of habit, but they were given nothing – neither words nor drink nor food. Suddenly a girl the same height as the cast-off military padded jacket she was wearing pushed her way through the queue of grown-up freeloaders – outcasts and people who'd succumbed to alcoholism, judging by their looks, as well as a few neatly-dressed, impoverished old women – to reach the funeral spread. Her loose coal-black hair covered her down to the shoulders like a headscarf. The wild, swarthy little face, peeking out like an old woman's, was puckered in an anguished grimace. Poking the backs of those sitting at the table, the girl said in a gruff, gravelly voice: 'Gimme some food . . . Gimme money for bread . . . '

Without a glance, they elbowed away the beggar who was bothering them. The little girl took no offence; she merely seemed surprised that so many people had assembled to eat, their backs turned as though rejecting her alone. She stopped, happy nevertheless to be at the front of the queue, stealing glances at the food. She hungrily fancied the big strange table was heaped with the most delicious and fragrant victuals. And, although she was begging for bread, when she spotted the plates smeared with leftovers, her powers of imagination imposed upon them the sweetest of grapes, the most luscious honeycombs of melons, steaming hunks of boiled mutton – all the foods that she had ever eaten once upon a time. The contemplation of this mirage was lulling her into a pleasant slumber and, already exhausted, she was yearning to curl up and sleep. But something kept on poking her in the side. The girl opened her eyes, all gummy from dozing, and was disgruntled to see someone's outstretched hand, apparently asking her for alms. She threw a disapproving look at the beggar sitting at the table, who turned out to be a soldier, without noticing the chocolate bar peeping out from the greatcoat sleeve that hid almost the whole of the man's hand.

When she realised it was a soldier, the beggar girl almost brightened up, parting her sulky lips, but the smile quickly vanished from her little face when she saw Kholmogorov grinning. This soldier resembled a scarecrow – he even smiled like some pauper or freak who was badgering people and grovelling. In her eyes, all those people called 'Russians' were stupid and greedy. They were stupid because it was easy to trick them and greedy because they only ever pulled a few pennies out of their pockets. In her little soul, she held all Russians in contempt. And right now, in her hungry somnolence and indifference she could not understand what one of them might be wanting from her. These goings-on did not escape the beady notice, however, of the pancake widow. Shaking her breasts in the air as if waving two fists, the colonel's wife pounced on Alyosha with a yell: 'Don't do it, don't give her anything! Shoo her away! She could have lice! Ugh, there's no rest from these refugees, the brazen little blighters. Back home they make children like there's no tomorrow, and then they arrive here and expect us to feed them!'

'Prostitute!' called out the little person in the soldier's padded jacket, glancing about amid the stupid and greedy folk looking on from every direction. The insulted colonel's wife took fright and went limp. The girl's breathing quickened, like a cornered animal waiting for death, although the guests stared at her indifferently and understood little in their drunken blur. She shouted something desperately and angrily, cursing in her own language this other people that had brought her nothing but fear and shame, then suddenly she threw herself under the protection of the soldier and, to everybody's amusement, flung her arms around him with all her passion, almost like a woman in love – which was what made it funny. The colonel's wife at first could not squeeze out even a murmur, and tears streamed from her painted, doll-like eyes. Her mascara ran, making two inky-blue spots appear beneath them. 'Me? *You* calling *me* a prostitute? Me?' She moaned in a trembling voice, as though she had been punched. The little beggar girl, in dread of whom this grown-up housewifely woman seemed to be shuddering with her entire being, suddenly stuck out her face, bared her teeth and, clinging to Kholmogorov, no longer afraid of anything in the world, she disgraced the colonel's wife with the same word again.

The colonel's wife began to sob and, before making herself scarce, she screeched at the guests, 'You didn't mind eating my whorish pancakes though, did you? You weren't too prudish for that. Oh, I know who's been spreading dirty stories about me . . . Well, I know what she is! You'd think she's all educated and skinny and refined! I might not be skinny like her, I don't know how to waggle the parts that she waggles, but for all that, my kids come from my husband, they all have a father, they're all clean and fed and healthy. I am an honest woman . . . I might happen to be temporarily divorced, but I'm never up for any Tom, Dick or Harry. I'm waiting for Mr Right, for love with a capital 'L', while she goes abandoning her child and running around the carriages, the bitch. She even smells like one. She might even have already caught lice from it. Look, her knickers might be crawling with them . . . ' She grabbed Mukhin's father by the lapels. 'Albert Gennadievich, you invited me to the wake, and I brought my pancakes along, and they've insulted me here. Albert Gennadievich, you rotter! I want nothing to do with you after this!'

The drunken man meekly allowed himself to be shaken and called a rotter, remaining torpidly silent. Once she had leapt like a shot from the funeral table, this time not as if she'd been punched but as though she were naked, timidly hiding her entirety in her own convulsive embrace, Mukhin's father must have sensed the cold empty space beside him for he said longingly: 'What a woman. What a woman!' A minute later, a plaintive babble had started up again around the table. Everybody continued their arguments. The little lass clambered onto the soldier's lap – urging him to help, as though he were a bit dense – and when she had sat down, she sneaked the chocolate bar from him, hid it quietly, slyly asked for another, and hid that one too.

'It's bad that you swear. Girls shouldn't use swear words,' Kholmogorov said. She clamped her lips moodily, slipped from his lap – and off she toddled like a goose, probably heading back where she'd come from.

When the beggar girl had vanished into the gloom of the third-class carriage, Alyosha began worrying that he'd offended her, and he pined and wilted, imagining how weak and hungry she was.

Some time elapsed. Suddenly something soft and light touched his back: it was the beggar girl pressing gently against him, making sure that it was the right man and he hadn't forgotten her, and pretending that she hadn't gone anywhere but had remained by his side. Craning her lithe neck, she drew closer to the swarming sounds of the arguing voices and listened earnestly, peering into the faces with her enquiring, understanding eyes, unable to tear them away even for a moment, as though she were not a witness but a judge.

'Ah, so you're back . . . ' Alyosha said, feeling forgiven. She heard this and gazed at him with the same piercingly tender look – then laughed, pleased with herself, thinking that this clumsy, kind-hearted man must be taken with her beauty. At last reassured that he had not gone anywhere, she grabbed the soldier's greatcoat sleeve as though she wanted to climb up Alyosha's arm like a monkey.

Alyosha endured all this. The girl started laughing again, because he was puffing and straining to support her weight, and she marvelled at herself: 'Huh, see how heavy I am!' Then she tugged his arm forcefully towards her, so that Kholmogorov had to surrender, and then, probably hoping for admiration, she said, 'Look how strong I am!' Feeling good, the girl whispered, 'Can I say a swear word, only to you, really quietly?' Sitting on the soldier's lap, she pressed against him to get even closer and whispered it, proud of doing something grown-ups do. He could not see her face, merely feeling a warm and even breathing somewhere on his temple. He listened meekly. And she became bored, as though she were playing all on her own. She immediately forgot everything and started babbling away: 'I know lots of soldiers! It was soldiers that brought us here. The soldiers gave us food and drink, and my padded jacket, and tablets . . . Have you got a gun? All soldiers have guns, I've seen them. Where's your gun? Where is it?'

As though he were required to come up with a fairy tale, Kholmogorov invented: 'I have an assault rifle, but I forgot to bring it with me.'

'You can kill!' said the girl in delight.

Alyosha mumbled, 'It's very bad when they shoot at people with assault rifles. Why don't you sit down and eat – you wanted to eat, didn't you?'

'Then why do you have a gun?' the little beggar girl stubbornly probed. He said nothing and the girl frowned but, in spite of her anger, she wriggled back into her soldier's lap for her treats. Once again she crammed all the booty into the pockets of her padded jacket, as though feeding their ravenous mouths with chocolate and hunks of bread.

This time she was hoarding almost without zeal, although she left the funeral table with her pockets bulging like bellies. She did not believe Kholmogorov: she thought that he had shot at people, and now he was lying. Wearily getting ready to head off somewhere again, she said, 'I'll come back to you, and we'll drink tea. This train isn't leaving, I know that; you can just come and go.'

In the dim light, they sipped hot tea served by the conductor. Everybody was speaking lifelessly about their own matters, and some places at the table already lay empty. Mukhin's father had nodded off in the same pose he'd adopted for his grieving: snuggled against the table, which he was hugging with arms that had stiffened over the hours and were arranged like a woodpile, atop of which lay, as though on the executioner's block, his dirty greying head. Somebody else, though, was rousing those around him with reckless gaiety, pestering and hectoring them one and all: his bodyguard Pavel Pavlovich, also known as Rafael. He left no one in peace – he was having fun, so everybody had to have fun, whether they liked it or not, especially the poor drunken lady whom he kept by his side, laughing and calling her Helen of

Troy, making her eat out of his hands, giving her squeezes under the table. She brushed him away petulantly, but was not in a fit state to summon up any intelligible phrases. The conductor was walking about the carriage all alone, bearing glasses of tea, and, in the intervals as he waited patiently for people to request a glass, he sat down by the dozing and equally lonely nuclear engineer, as though silently conversing with him. He was as buoyant as though he were at work, yet filled with such serenity that he was willing to serve his tea for free, never flagging nor losing his cheer. He enjoyed sitting next to Mukhin's father, who may have been asleep, yet even so, it felt as though he were serving that amazing man, one of a kind. He liked carrying the glasses through the sleepless night-time carriage. He loved being surrounded by trusted and reliable persons. And he enjoyed the densely steaming hot water filling the glasses, and the juice released in the swirling brew, the price of which he didn't know. He would usually take whatever he was offered for a glass of tea; for some reason this was the only way he could work. Tea had vanished from the shop shelves a year ago. He had heard on the radio that the whole country had run out of tea. Stolen by somebody from somewhere, those tightly-filled packets of tea had been bartered for the conductor's freebie coal, which in effect was pilfered too, as he was heating the carriage-hotel more frugally. In this way he cared for the boarders, believing that for them hot tea always came first, just as it did for passengers on a journey.

'Give us two glasses of tea without sugar,' the girl said importantly upon her return, and the sturdy man happily came to life. 'It shall be done, mistress. Two glasses of tea with sugar!' he commanded himself, and ran off for it.

Kholmogorov was not overjoyed at the beggar girl's return. He even took fright as she clambered onto his lap, wanting to sit just so at the table. He could not have done anything to hurt her, but already he was pining and wilting at the closeness of this strange little street girl who was old beyond her years, sensing a certain shame that had arrived along with her. Seeing that the table was empty in front of the girl, Pavel Pavlovich flew into a rage and shouted, 'What bastards, you couldn't spare some grub for her! Hey, little sister, we'll take it all away from them – you've got to eat, you still need to grow, unlike them. They'll kick the bucket tomorrow. See? All of it's for you! Eat up and don't let anyone else have any.' He swept everything edible on the table into the corner where the girl was sitting on Kholmogorov's lap and said menacingly, 'Listen, don't do anything to upset my little sister, or I'll bite off your noses! She's the only one here who can tell me what to do. You all got it? Tuck in, little sister, eat your fill, I said! Anyone touches her – I'll kill them!'

The girl stayed silent – this soldier frightened her, and he seemed even stupider and greedier than all the people whose food he had taken for her. When he had turned and left them alone, she moved the plate away – back towards the guests from whom he'd taken it. She kept just a few pieces for herself – and put aside the same amount again for Alyosha. Afterwards she was quiet for a while and then gave voice to what must have been troubling her: 'He's a very bad man. Why did you let him yell at you? I'll kill him myself if I can find a gun.'

Kholmogorov did not know what to say in response. He asked, 'What's your name?'

'Aidym.'

'Aidym?' Kholmogorov asked in order to have something to talk about. 'It's like our word for smoke.'

'And you're like a camel!' she said gruffly and scornfully. 'Is that what you're called? We have to drink tea. I love tea. At home we all drank lots and lots of tea. Do you have your own home?'

'Yes . . . Tomorrow I'm catching the train and going home.' The girl frowned.

'Will your train go far away?' she asked faintly, as though for some reason she was ashamed of asking. Alyosha became pleasantly lost in thought, reminiscing about home, and he spent a long time speaking as though he were already sitting in the train carriage, travelling blissfully for days and nights on his way home. Aidym listened carefully, gazing at the troubled face disfigured by its squirmy smile as though by a scar, for a long while unable to tear away her understanding, inquisitive eyes, and then suddenly she stopped the soldier short by saying, 'I'm going to be your wife.'

'What's this? Do it, Lyosha, get married! At least I'll get to party one last time! My soul is all shook up, how can you not see that?' Pavel Pavlovich's words rang over the table in a joyous tormented howl. 'You won't find a better bride than my sister, don't even think of it. We orphans know how to love! Oooh! Heart nailed to heart, that's what it's like, our love. Or maybe you think she's not good enough for you? Forget the fact that she's dressed like a scarecrow . . . She's pure gold, this little girl, with a diamond inside her, I'm telling you. Oh marry her, you fool, for God's sake I beg you! Ugh, the devil with this, I'm all out of patience . . . Right, once and for all, in the name of all powers, the Devil and God, death and life, I pronounce you, little sister and little brother, husband and wife! What are you gawping at, you bastards? Don't you like it? You were guests at a wake – and now it's a celebration; you're all wedding guests, got it? So rejoice, or I'll kill you!' And he yelled at the top of his voice: 'Kiss the bride! Kiss the bride!' With the same energy pumping through his soul, Pavel Pavlovich suddenly grabbed his own lady, already dishevelled from his courtship, pulled her into an embrace and planted a kiss on her lips, which were clenched with fear. It was a defiantly long kiss. The guests were petrified, but they managed to come up with some smiles and giggles. A minute later, Yelena had come back to life. Her wooden little arms and legs that had protruded from her boa-constricted female body began twitching again. Plaintive moans became audible through her closed lips. But this first kiss taken from her merely stirred his desire for more. Tormenting her breezily and deliberately, he bellowed into her groaning mouth, feigning wild passion. Again she went limp in his arms – magnanimously he stopped the torture. When he let go of her, she tumbled out of his arms like a corpse, her face a mask with a hole cut out for the mouth, which was hot and plump, with crimson petal lips. The lips were moving: 'Let me go . . . Help . . . '

'It's too late to make out you're a non-smoker,' her tormentor grinned, pleased with himself. 'We'll just smoke one little ciggie each and you can run home to Mummy and Daddy . . . I'll give you an entire sea of love and flowers – you did say that was what you wanted!'

Hiding her face, Aidym was wheezing hoarsely into the soldier's greatcoat, snuggling into its manly folds. Kholmogorov himself was staring at his workmate, completely lost. Alyosha had heard Pavel Pavlovich giving himself a new name, but he had been waiting meekly for him to start speaking like his old self again. The new hero, however, was blissfully happy. He was spread out on a bunk, one arm hung like a horse collar around the neck of his lady, who was still gasping for air, while with the other he was conducting the guests with a grin. Compliantly, they raised a few toasts. Then he felt like singing and began to drawl in a gravelly voice:

> *The blue carriage is chugging along,*
> *Rolling along,*
> *The express train is picking up steam . . .*

When he heard no one joining in, he pulled a ferocious face that implied: 'Sing it, or I'll kill you.' The guests warbled the chorus discordantly in forlorn and childish voices: '*Oh, what a pity it will all end now.*' And he was soloing on, rapt, his eyes filling with tears and narrowing in languor.

Alyosha joined in too, like everyone else. He was used to obeying his mysterious companion. He was pining for at least a little kindness. He could have not remembered the words or the tune: despite hearing the song often as a child, he didn't think he'd heard it since, and it seemed long forgotten. But suddenly he began belting it out, cawing along with everyone else as though they were lined up in ranks, frightful for anyone with an ear for music but loud and in unison.

When her soldier began singing, the girl went quiet, listening to the steady, deep, stove-like boom in his chest. She had been frightened and angry but now she became calm and happy. Kholmogorov felt the stifling heaviness present when Aidym was wheezing and crossly pushing against him had been lifted from his soul. His chest filled with a pleasant tingling warmth like cotton wool. In fact this must have come over Alyosha while he was joyously lost in singing as loud as he could. Meanwhile Aidym's clingy nimble little hands were scrambling about the soldier's coat like spiders, stealing into all the pockets in turn, rummaging about their unexpected emptiness . . . Not finding what she'd been thinking of, Aidym grew timid in sheer happiness: knowing that within the soldier's greatcoat there had to be even more pockets than on the outside, the girl didn't dare come too close to his body. She lost hope of weaving her web and withdrew her hands. And without knowing the words to the strange Russian song, she began to join in, crooning it gently:

> *The journey's unfurling like a tablecloth,*
> *Stretching away to the distant sun,*
> *Everyone, everyone . . . Is hoping for the best!*

The wedding was in full swing. To the strains of this happy sadness, in the dim light of the third-class carriage, Mukhin's father revived.

His dull, sleepy eyes were bulging like a fish's; taking umbrage, he surveyed the goings-on. He sat gazing deafly at the singing mouths, unable to make out what time or place he had found himself in. The only thing he took in, with a disgust that was also somehow fishlike, was that he was among people. Landed on shore, dazed by the sensation of his own sobriety, Mukhin's father was returning to life with sporadic breaths in and out and his eyes remained open. He was gulping in air, but it wasn't quenching his thirst. Right before him in grieving silence stood the two tumblers of vodka that shone like lead. They were pinned down with the same two slices of black bread, which over the hours had become stale and turned blacker still.

'Dad's back,' cordially noted Pavel Pavlovich, also known as Rafael, straightening up at the table. 'Come on then, tell us where you've been, what exploits you got up to. I love a good fairy tale. You know what it's like: so boring, nothing ever changes, makes you want to scream. But you want things to be the way they never are. Well it's not like that's a question. Do I know or don't I? – Now that's a question! And the thing is, I do know, I do . . . Ha! Now tell me, why is there no precision to life? Why won't you say something? You thought up your fairy tale, but you can't make head nor tail of your own life, or so you'd have us believe. Ah, but you will make sense of it; that's what I've risked my hide for. I was watching and watching you, standing to attention there on the platform, and I thought to myself, *It's not right!* See, I know who shot him, Dad; the driver always knows everything about everybody. Beginning to guess what a tale we've got here? And you too are about to find out what kind of death your son met. You might not want to, but you will. You'll find it all out!'

Mukhin's father remained silent, staring at a single point the whole time. It was as though he had been whacked on the back with a stick, which had merely made him stretch out jerkily to full height. 'Oh, you're back to standing to attention, are you . . . I ought to flatten you . . . I'm sick of this . . . Are you a worm or a man?' This time the man's eyes, piercing in their pain, darted right at their target, with the result that Pavel Pavlovich, also known as Rafael, came to his senses and went silent.

Suddenly the little man found his tongue, saying glumly, 'Where's my hat?'

'Dad, oh Dad . . . What kind of a man are you! Your hat's gone. You left it and went for a stroll,' the soldier said, softening.

'Who are you?' came the second question.

'You can think of me as a hello from the land of the dead. I was sent by Gennady Mukhin to whisper something to you: ever heard of him? Your beloved son? Thing is, he wasn't no hero . . . Seems he was shot by an officer, his own commander, because the guy felt like it. Had a pistol in his holster. Power's too mild a word for it! You want to execute them? Just do it. Want to pardon them? Do it – like God Himself. Fingers get itchy, he freaks out – that's when he went to fire, drew his pistol from the holster. Now he's resting his nerves in the infirmary, because that's how it has to be. And your son is going to feed the worms in a zinc jacket because that's how it has to be. And all everybody cares about is hurrying things up, choosing the fastest train, just so life can carry on! So, their births are a mistake, their lives are a mistake – everything's all a mistake. Now one mistake got corrected. And you're correcting another one, you bastard, while you're guzzling your vodka . . . And I am too; all of us are. Isn't life sickening!'

Silence opened again like a chasm, audible down to the teeniest creak, the slightest rustle. People began wriggling. On the upper berths they were all listening, but instantly pretended to be asleep. 'Rafael . . . Rafael . . . ' mumbled the lady in her stupor, then suddenly began snoring unpleasantly. Night entered the third-class carriage the way a strange wilderness and darkness must creep into a tightly sealed coffin deep below the ground. One of the guests sitting on the fringes jumped up and fled. Somebody giggled. It was stifling.

'Anyone for tea?' The conductor began to fuss. Mukhin's father grabbed one of the glasses in front of him that still held vodka and quickly drained it.

'What are we going to do?' Alyosha said in surprise, looking around, unable to make sense of it all.

'Now keep calm, the train's on schedule. Don't you fuss, skin-and-bones, you can hop off at the right moment. It's easy enough. Your ticket to life's journey won't expire. The important thing is you have nothing to do with it, now remember that. It's me who has no stops, just a one-way ticket, and the road is as round as a wheel. I sometimes take pity on other people, but when it comes to myself, I'll jump right into the fire. Maybe I just can't feel pain, I've grown used to it. I can stub out cigarettes on my tongue, drive a nail into myself anywhere – it doesn't hurt and I don't feel sorry for myself. All well and good, I'll just go along on my ride. Can't you all sing me something, then? A farewell song? That would be nice! You don't want to? Too proud? Then I'll sing on my own . . . You don't love me? Well I don't love you either, but I'll still sing you something, oh how I'll sing, while you'll just sit there pitying yourselves.'

This time the guests in the third-class carriage did not even know the words or tune to the mournful orphan's song that Pavel Pavlovich was singing in a drawl; he was as alien to them as a waif. No matter how much spirit he put into it, his solitary voice could not rise to the occasion. He was warbling slightly off-key, as if pretending to sing while in fact wishing to throw open his soul, to get closer to people, rather than being phoney and insincere yet again. But he mustered the courage, or some unexpected powers of humility, perhaps, to keep drawing out the boastful, syrupy sounds that were torturous, even for him. The guests were overcome with apathy and impotence. They listened unwillingly, motionless, shackled by this pause that had occurred in their lives.

It lasted a long time, and the air in this third-class bay became charged with a sour fustiness, like a squat little button battery filling with electricity, from the breathing of this one person.

Pavel Pavlovich's voice trembled, grew quieter and then broke off when, growing nearer and louder as though through the depths of non-existence, forcing its way towards the people in the third-class carriage, there came a knocking. Right up close, just below the train windows, a muffled, dull drumming of feet was advancing in bounds along the earth. A solitary yell rang out, harsh and distinct; it must have been some command, followed by a sinister baying of dogs rushing to maul the air. Everybody listened in shock. A furious thudding of boots burst into the emptiness of the carriage. A wild clamouring shout came rushing towards them: 'Police!' But in the scrum raging in the narrow neck of the carriage, figures cocooned in army greatcoats became discernible. The ray of an angry torch, perhaps of many, with pupils like headlamps, was blinding and scouring the faces in full beam. They scorched the eyes even more harshly. The powerful united wave of the raid crashed down on the funeral-table barricade. The boards went flying: some lodging in sheets or jabbing like spikes into people; others snapping with a gunshot crack under their own pressure. Crockery rained down, screeching in the crush underfoot. Suddenly a jubilant cry rang out – perhaps it was 'Collar 'em, my friends,' or it could have been 'Collar my friends'. A few moments later, out of the roaring, crashing and shrieking rose a deathly howl.

There was a pause, and then the call was relayed through the carriage: 'Somebody's been knifed!' – 'Help!' – 'Give us some frigging light here!' – 'He's alive!'

The wounded man – for he was still alive – was carried out of the carriage like a sack of potatoes. People were hurrying as if a fire had broken out. For the first ten minutes or so, while everyone was wailing in the chaos of the raid, panic reigned. Perhaps in the hope of saving him, perhaps of saving themselves, they dragged away the man's limp, heavy body, its clothing erupting before their eyes in a blaze of red. They ended up with him in the dark on a bare, dank patch outside the carriage. Not knowing where to run or what to do, they were carrying him suspended by his arms and legs, because they would have had to hunt around even to find a stretcher. The two military policemen were losing their grip. The body was beginning to slip from their hands, drooping and falling as though into a hole. The man was moaning in pain and humiliation, feeling forgotten. Then he mustered the strength to snivel, for he wanted to live: 'Where's the ambulance? My friends! Do something . . . What are you doing? I'm in pain . . . For crying out loud, I'm dying!' The senior in the patrol grew fed up of this whining and said angrily, as though cursing, 'Oh put him down, I'm sick of this!'

The bleeding man didn't know what this all meant, but he was soothed to feel that he was lying stretched out on his back, impervious to the cold ground onto which he'd been lowered. The military policemen urgently sought help at the scene, but in vain. They were searching for cotton wool and bandages. To plug the wound, which was leaking blood, they would at least need to pull out the murder weapon. Still sticking in the man's chest was the fatal sharpened iron spike that had been plunged to an unknown depth with uncertain danger, but it was in to the hilt. Seeing all this, the senior soldier became afraid to shoulder the responsibility. Awoken and afraid, people began pouring out of the carriages. There was no medical worker of any description to be found in the crowd of onlookers. It soon became clear that this dosshouse-on-wheels was utterly disconnected from the world. A runner was sent to the station to phone for an ambulance. The soldier ran for help as fast as his legs could carry him, or perhaps he dawdled, but on his return they again waited in vain. The ambulance that was called out could not find the entrance to the right dead end. Or maybe they had got lost somewhere else. Maybe they had turned back ages ago.

The crowd at the scene of the incident straggled into the carriages to go back to bed. The senior in the patrol was warming himself in the very carriage where they had caught the two young soldiers who had gone AWOL from their commanding officer. One of those soldiers had by that time been identified as the commanding officer's killer. They were now waiting for the police to get there and register the deserters. The runner had been sent back to the station, this time to fetch the police.

Three bodies now lay prostrate outside the carriage, under guard of the soldiers on military police duty, also left out in the wind and cold, surrounded by darkness. The two live ones were face down, their legs and arms splayed as if on a cross-frame. The dead one, whose arms and legs had been calmly folded, was facing skywards. They could see from his eyes that the Head of the Infirmary for the Karaganda Regiment had gone to meet his maker: they had completely glassed over – frosted like November mud at night, and glinting with the same surprised and icy shine. 'So I'm dead now?' those eyes seemed to be saying. 'How lousy this life is . . . What a lousy sky . . . ' From the trench coat which the corpse was wearing, unnoticed by anyone, crawled out a teensy little grey creature – not a mouse even, but a mouse pup that had remained for some unknown time hidden in the lining at the bottom of the coat. It crawled out – and quivered like a little heart, staring at the face of the man in front of it. The mouse pup didn't know anything and couldn't do anything, and it carried out the only meaningful movement of which it was capable, imprinted into its mind for the sake of hygiene, although now it seemed as though it were grieving and washing in tears, and then it became calm and scurried under the smelly carriage to freedom.

'Is this night ever going to end?' grumbled the chilly soldier who was on guard.

'Oh but it's morning already. And the afternoon is going to look like morning. And we've still got to lug the stiff about, no doubt . . . While those guys are lying there having a ball. Hey listen, you bastards, you're going to get the works! You'll be bathing in blood soon enough, you'll see,' the same guard said, letting off steam. But it clearly didn't help him feel better. He took a run of three or four steps and stuck his boot into one of the men on the ground.

Opening his eyes, he thought he had ceased to exist. His consciousness was reeling from the blows, and his body had ceased heeding its own pain. He must have been lying on the side where his rib was broken but coming to from the pain, he could not in any case move a muscle, not even to roll onto his back to ease the agony. Outside the railway carriage, fate had been kind to him: the punches had landed on the first man they found. Then the guards had puffed their chests out and led them as though into the future. The foreign little beggar girl in the soldier's padded jacket had traipsed after them in silence. The military police could not work out what she wanted. Needing to get rid of her little outsider's eyes, they chased her away. Then at a remote spot, a senior officer suddenly gave the command to stop: their fellow soldiers began beating them up again. Each tried to get in a strike; they were fired up and pummelling randomly with their fists. He endured it all meekly. The other man incurred their wrath by hitting a guard back. But he only managed to swing his fist into the guard once. They immediately knocked him down, encircled him and mired him in mud – not only was every inch of him now black and blue, but there wasn't a patch left clean. The officer had been smoking to one side, waiting: his simple, honest-looking face remained calm.

Seemingly absolved, Alyosha was now standing alongside the officer and began weeping as he watched the other man suffer. The officer found his tongue: 'That one won't cry. Be a hero if he went into intelligence.' He finished the cigarette and shouted, 'Right then, champions, break it up, he's had enough!' They left the doubled-up body on the ground and retreated; he was ordered to lift the body and haul it along. He happily clutched at his load, grappling to cope with it – and the other man clung to him as though for dear life, still muttering profanities through his pain, groans alternating with growled-out curses.

The journey of these two men, bound together by their respective convulsions, was brief. The soldiers handed the arrested men over to the guards: now they were prisoners. All the cells seemed to be empty, such was the silence. And this silence was quietly augmented by the two new arrivals, who were now separated.

Before entering the cell, he was searched. They ordered him to surrender his greatcoat and belt. He graciously carried this out, imagining that he was handing them his outer layer as a guest might when visiting. His hosts smiled cordially. He was left in the dead man's short tunic. Warmed by the welcome, he asked with a thoughtful and understanding look: 'Should I take my boots off?' They answered him with matching gravity: 'That's up to you; some do, some don't.' Then, of his own volition, he removed his footwear. Shielding their eyes and barely containing their laughter, they quickly appropriated the pair of lacquered orchestral boots. Nothing was left for them to covet. They opened up the cell and let their barefoot prisoner in as though he were a child, without telling him what would come next.

The door slammed behind him like a gunshot. The floor, walls and ceiling, all covered in the same bare concrete tiles, were frosted with white. He just stood there, unsure where to go. His eyes were wearily seeking some kind of warmth. The heat produced by his body was instantly spent on the air, which was so bitingly cold that breathing was painful. Just below the ceiling a small wolfish window was howling; through the aperture, laced with a web of bars, a meagre light from the sky filtered in. His gaze was drawn towards the light. The narrow, elongated cell was a little deeper than a grave. He shivered, his strength painfully ebbing away as though he were a dying ember, and stared in amazement at the light, just as near as it was far, offering him no help, not even warmth.

Here too they had their own justice. He would be beaten periodically by the guards coming on duty. The guards were rotated every two hours. They would enter the cell all smiles and kindness, and somewhat tiddly. To protect their hands, they'd wind a belt around their fists. When he caught on that they would use their fists while you were still standing, and once you'd fallen they'd set in with their boots, he started dropping to the ground. That way it would be over faster. At one point he called out, already half-senseless from the drubbings: 'Where am I?' And he heard the reply: 'Where are you? Karaganda or Timbuktu?' Then, forgetting himself, he implored, 'What have I ever done to you?' They merely laughed in reply. They were aware that the newcomers had been picked up for murder. Until they dispatched such men to the prison camps, they would dutifully inflict torment on them here. And this torture continued the whole time, and he lost track of time, no longer sure whether he'd been there for a day or for days and nights on end.

His soul seemed either to be seeking the path to salvation or, perhaps, it was making some final farewell round. He saw everything that had happened over the many years, but not the way it had really been: good and bad, the faces of his loved ones – and all he had done in secret from them. Everything combined beyond time, in separate sequences, each in turn. And it was this sudden realisation that terrified him: everything was flashing past, never to be repeated. His soul desperately clung to the higgledy-piggledy images and sensations from his past life, from a time when he had simply been free, and he wept not from fear or pain but from envy for the person he had been, as though it were a different man who had been given his life and even his face. And that man was to live in his place, breathing and drinking. That man would go as a son to his father and mother's house, and they'd love him until their dying day. And he began babbling, as he had in childhood, unable to stay mute any longer, sensing only the icy concrete tiles beneath him: 'I won't do it again. I'm sorry, please, forgive me . . . I'll be good as gold.' He would sink from exhaustion into some black space, but he had merely to wake and again he'd start mumbling, unable to believe that he would never find forgiveness.

'Hey, still not got it?' a shout rang out again. 'You were told to leave the cell, you bastard. You can play stupid once you're in the investigator's office.' The guard stood aloof at the door. He closed his eyes and opened them: the guard had not moved. Nearby stood some boots. They were army boots, a knackered old pair, to replace the ones that had vanished.

'Hello, son, take a seat,' said a woman in a neat, humble uniform. She was sitting behind a steel table sunk into the floor, diligently continuing to write, and for a long while she paid him no further attention. She was in her early forties. Her face was softly encircled with a pleasant firm plumpness. Her hair was tied back simply with a clip. Her eyes jealously followed the words that were issuing from her hand and then roving, as if guilty of something, to the edge of the white sheet. Writing did not come easily to this woman, but she enjoyed making all those words obey her and line up in rows. When she pressed down firmly on the pen, her face also pulsed with stress, adopting an intently cruel look. For no other reason than to help the man brought for interview shorten the time spent in her office – which was like a cell in appearance, though tangibly filled with her womanly calm, warmth and quiet – the boss spoke gruffly and with a sternness befitting the questions. 'Tell me how you fell into the company of a man like Nazeikin. Who fatally stabbed the head of the infirmary? Whose idea was it? Who did the bladed instrument belong to?' When no answer was forthcoming, she sighed: 'Fine. Don't say anything. But I know anyway.' His head was aching with every word. He did not speak because he could not recall anyone in his life with that name. The boss began writing as though taking dictation from herself, without lifting her gaze from the table, 'The fingerprints found on the bladed instrument entirely match those of Nazeikin. The witness statements taken from the patrol group say that the attack was delivered by Nazeikin. Being in a state of severe alcoholic intoxication, Nazeikin pulled out the bladed instrument and dealt a single blow to the heart; the outcome was fatal. And where were you when all this happened? What were you doing to stop it? Both of you refused to carry out your commanding officer's orders. Both of you walked off without authorisation. Both of you consumed alcohol on that fateful night. The patrol group claimed you and Nazeikin both resisted arrest together. So evil was committed. And evil must be punished.'

She seemed to add a full stop – and she was done. She pushed the report aside. Somewhat awkwardly she pulled out from under the table a bottle of *kefir* and a bun flecked with raisins, all tucked up in a clean white cloth. The distraught appearance of the detainee, who could easily have passed for a victim of crime, did not disconcert her in the slightest. She began chewing intently and moodily, as though performing yet another laborious duty. She swallowed a mouthful and washed it down with some *kefir* from the bottle, whitening her lips with the nourishing milky liquid. Suddenly her face brightened with surprise and she said in a clear voice, 'Here, have some.' But then she frowned, wiped her lips with the cloth, took a bite of the bun and asked indifferently, 'Maybe you'd like some? Ok, then, don't say anything. Hey, guards, come on guys! Who's there? Artur, sweetheart, come here.' The guard who had brought him in for questioning arrived in the office. In a businesslike tone, though with her mouth full, she mumbled, 'Now bring me Anatoli Nazeikin. Huh, it won't be for the first time. And have this one washed, shaved and fed, find him something decent to eat and return all his things to him. I want him all cleaned up and shipshape. Then bring him back here and call me out into the corridor.'

'Yes ma'am, Svetlana Ivanovna!' the guard responded promptly, gazing at her in admiration.

'Good, I'm glad it's all good . . . ' she answered, into empti-ness. Now alone in the office, she sat placidly and chewed on her bun, which had such a paucity of raisins that she had to wait a long time for each burst of sweetness in her mouth, like waiting for wishes to be fulfilled. 'Eat from your bowl, don't listen to a soul,' she said to someone who wasn't there, unless it was to herself – and she suddenly seemed an old woman.

When she had filled her belly, she got up from the table, carefully pulling her swollen stomach out from under it before rising. She stretched her arms out wide, and from her unbuttoned jacket protruded the entire life-giving orb of her own flesh and blood. She gave a yawn and waddled over to the wall where you could see the sky through the muzzle of bars. Gazing wistfully at the dim light of the sky, she stroked her stomach a few times. She sighed patiently, thinking of her due date. Then she carried her stomach back to her workplace, already thinking of the murder case, for which she still had to extract a confession out of the perpetrator. And she retreated within her four prison walls.

The guard had seen a lot, but this was the first time he had taken a prisoner straight from interrogation to have a shower. It was oppressive to think about, somehow. To lend your razor – let alone to shave – a man whom you had beaten and robbed: it was so repulsive that his hands rebelled. But half an hour later the newborn man, his shining wet hair slicked into a middle parting and smooth face already dry, was sitting in the guardroom as though he were one of them, waiting to be taken and fed. He suddenly spotted two soldiers pushing a man shackled in handcuffs down the corridor. The man was refusing to budge and cursing greedily, craning over his shoulder to see their faces.

His gaze must have been piercing. The guards were ill at ease. They couldn't manage a swipe at him nor shout him into submission even though there were two of them. They laboured in silence, sweating and puffing. They were shoving him along with jabs, but it felt as though he were pushing them back and looked almost as if it were he who was shoving them. There was everything in him: a furious sensation of his own strength, a hunger for power over these people, which at that moment could only have been assuaged by their blood. The only thing missing was any hope of escape. But freedom shot through him like lightning and shrieked in his throat when, beside himself with joy at the sight of the man who sat waiting, he yelled: 'Alyosha!' Thinking he saw his friend rushing to his aid from the far end of the corridor, he surged forward – not towards him, but ramming his shackled body into the stunned guards. But as soon as they realised what was happening, brought to their senses by the yell, which had vanished into nothingness, they acted swiftly: one of them grabbed him by the hair and immediately bent him backwards with relish as though turning him inside out, the other punched him in the stomach, making him buckle and collapse to his knees.

Without allowing him to get his wind, they grabbed him under the armpit on each side and dragged him along. But even hanging limply as they hauled him along, he seemed to be fighting, angrily butting his forehead against the empty air. He could not take in the fact this was only happening to him. As he writhed in agony, he called out: 'Lyoshka, hang on in there! Our time will come . . . Just give it time, we'll get out. We'll do them . . . ' And then he groaned a bit and commanded himself with all his might: 'A death for a death!'

The guard returned, out of breath and surly, and led him to the dining area. He barked, 'Surname?'

The answer came as a belated moan: 'Hlmuorov.'

He suddenly added gruffly: 'I reckon you're a grass. Sold your friend down the river, did you?'

When he had ladled a bowl of barley porridge from the army pot, he shoved it towards him: 'There, eat!' But the man who he thought had betrayed his comrade for a bowl of porridge for some reason would not touch the food. 'I told you to eat.'

'Uh-uh.'

'Lost your appetite? Wouldn't mind giving you a good pummelling. Don't worry, we'll do it once you're back in the cell.' All the men who had come off duty came to gawp at the informer. 'We've already tidied up his teeth a bit.' 'There's a Judas for you.' 'You've wasted your time washing and shaving, 'cause you're a dead man. Better just go and hang yourself.' They couldn't force him to eat for fear of consequences from on high – they'd get porridge all over him. Then the guard remembered the order to smarten the prisoner up: after a quick think, they told him to take off his boots, then they put him in front of a rusting basin to wash them. Without a brush or even a cloth, it was a case of cleaning them by hand. This they could make him do, jabbing his side, reawakening his still painful wound. The boots now shone, but they shoved him again: 'Come on, get them cleaner, Judas!' And when they got to his coat, which they had been ordered to return, they made him pluck off by hand all the mud that had stuck, even the tiny specks.

An hour must have passed, if not more. They still had to take the prisoner back for interrogation. Outside the doors to the office, the guard suddenly hesitated: an angry female shout was coming from the investigator's room. 'Hey, don't you treat me like that. Svetlana Ivanovna Svetikova is a human being! And you, you piece of trash, are getting her worked up. Right, I've had it. You're a dead man. I'm sick of this. We'll rid the earth of your presence tonight.' The guard knocked and opened the door, without waiting for permission. Shouts burst forth: 'Sign the interview record, you fucker, or I'll make you eat it . . . ' The woman's distorted face could be seen in the doorway. Risen from her chair in fury, she was wielding a scrawl-covered sheet like a sabre over the head of the man sitting across the table. Only his back was visible, but it was hunched and somehow remote, as though it were part of an already decapitated body that for some reason had been set on a chair.

The boss stopped the interrogation and left the office. She examined the prisoner from head to foot and, pleased with his appearance, she sent the guard away. Firmly and authoritatively, she said, 'Follow me!' One after the other, doors swung open, and it became more light and airy. 'I shall lean on you. I am expecting, you know; it's hard for me to do things alone. I just want it to be over. You're lucky that your case came to me, seeing as Nazeikin has outdone himself this time. Be thankful you had someone to plead for you. One thing I've noticed in my time is that if a man's willing to sacrifice everything and fight tooth and nail, he'll save his loved ones. But the type who just mumble and grumble are wasting their time camping on your doorstep – their kith and kin have had it.' She stopped and recovered her breath. They must have come to the last door. She pulled his military ID out of her jacket pocket. Returning it to him, she said: 'If you had any cash with you, don't try getting it back. Well, you're demobbed and can make your way home now. You saw nothing and you don't know anyone. You weren't in this town yesterday or today, got it?' Suddenly she shouted harshly, 'Or do you want to go back inside?' He smiled and kept a guilty silence, not realising that the boss would have been all too happy to have him back. 'Oy, what's all this? They took your gold teeth?' she said, gasping and in a lather. Something made him shake his head in happy denial. 'Well, just resign yourself to it, son; you'll live. And as for your teeth – once you're out you can fit yourself up with all the teeth you like, even gold ones.'

He did not understand that he was being released. When it happened, he took fright: they opened the steel door – and suddenly he was standing in a clean, deserted street, with nowhere to go. His benumbed legs were gently buckling, and in his head he could hear the boss's whining voice, now directed at the man to whom he was being transferred right outside the gates of the building, with its outer bricks as red as blood.

His keeper was deaf and seemed unable to believe that he was looking at the very person whom he'd recalled so lovingly as a son all this time, though he had not dreamt that he'd set eyes on him again when he'd seen him off to his native parts, already imagining him with his eternal tooth. 'Why did you do it?' the man seemed to be asking with heartbroken eyes. He stood there, realising that it was Abdulla Ibrahimovich who had come for him, but he could not speak. He was silent. The deaf man gazed hard at him, waiting in distress for an answer, some movement of the lips. He shouted as though fearful that he had just lost his hearing: 'What did you say?

What are you saying?' Seeing a smile that bared some black wounds in place of the teeth, he shrank back in silence.

Abdullayev began walking without looking back. He set off timidly behind Abdulka, tailing along and probably hoping for forgiveness, but for the whole journey he seemed intentionally to be lagging behind. As they walked through the streets, twilight descended. Everything unfamiliar and strange was seeing them off through the city until, in the cold and emptiness, the railway station emerged.

The waiting room was swarming with people and filled with light. Beyond the black mirrors of windows looking straight out to the platform, a distant roar could be heard. Women, men and children, who seemed to be seeking safety here, were jostling in their search for a place under the soaring empty vault. Or, finding a place, they were huddling: some against their luggage of prim, stumpy-nosed suitcases, in shades of black or brown; others against their belongings, which were bursting the sides of their bundles, or simply huddling against each other so as not to be lost. At the window to the military ticket office, there was space again to breathe. In this oasis of order and of a law distinct from that of the public queues, they were given upon request an outbound passenger seat on a train leaving at midnight.

Not far from the military ticket window a patrol group was standing about – a duty officer and two lads in officer cadet uniforms who smelled of aftershave. The officer took a closer look and his face darkened: the newly arrived passenger in hideous boots, who had something just as unsightly sticking out from the collar of his greatcoat and whose face had clearly taken a hammering, evinced such disgust that it was too late to ask him for his papers: this scarecrow was crying out for arrest. Abdulka shuddered at the officer's gaze and backed away, shielding the lad. The patrol group surrounded the two of them. The deaf man pulled the officer aside and whispered: 'Don't touch him, please. He's released on health grounds, he isn't right in the head. His train is coming soon. He's going home to be unwell.' The face of the duty officer, which had been intently morose, suddenly went soft and a little stupid: he believed this and gave an understanding nod, glancing over his shoulder in his desire to move away from this scarecrow of a soldier.

The patrol group retreated.

Abdulka had no further business in this city. With the look of someone who was staying behind, like a loving man with no one left to love, he was saying goodbye at the train station merely to an hour of his own life. His face was forbiddingly aloof. They spent this time together in the waiting room because the boss was waiting in the warmth for his commuter train home. Suddenly the deaf man whined to himself, not realising that the words could be heard: 'I wanted good for you. I treated you all well . . . ' And stony-faced, he suddenly fell silent. And when he looked for the last time, he said in a menacing voice: 'Don't follow me! I don't know you.'

He was left on his own, and the man who had so simply and brutally given him back his rescued life went away, this time for ever. Along with the ticket there was money in his pocket, ten roubles: a reddish-coloured note just as final – Abdulka's last sacrifice – as that last fierce gaze of his and his last words.

The unkempt and feral-looking soldier, who smiled like a monkey at everyone he met, soon attracted attention at the station: he looked as if he were searching lucklessly for something or someone. He showed up several times at the buffet, eyeing the same counter that looked like a bone picked clean. In the late evening, the only beverage available in the buffet was something labelled 'tea drink'. The lad asked for a glass of this tea and handed over his ten roubles in payment for this brew priced at a few kopecks. He drank it hungrily and left. When he turned up again, he asked firmly for a cup of tea. The swill was lukewarm but, standing to the side, he slurped on it for a long time, as though it were freshly boiled.

Something similar happened in the waiting room, where he took each seat in turn as they became vacant, but then happily gave them up to women with children or to the elderly. And on the platform too, he paced from end to end with an air of great importance, coming to the notice of all the people meeting or seeing off each new train as he enquired which train was arriving or departing and from which platform, and then reported this information to anyone standing open-mouthed or rushing to find out. As he passed the patrol, he tried as impressively as possible to salute the duty officer and seemed to be deliberately popping into their sight. Suddenly he went and asked for permission to make a call of nature, as though he were deserting his post. The officer was confused; nevertheless, timorously mirroring his seriousness, he personally gave him permission to do so, and even sent one of his cadets to show the way to the toilets. He addressed the officer again for permission to take a walk in the station forecourt – and they quickly tired of him. The officer brushed him away, telling him gruffly that he could go wherever he wanted. He returned to the waiting room carrying a huge watermelon, which at this time of night the Kazakhs had done well to sell him from their wind-battered nomadic stall that resembled a tent, awaiting late-night customers in the forecourt. Hugging the old and weighty watermelon he had bought unintentionally and to all appearances not for himself, he popped up again before the commander and reported that he'd purchased a watermelon. The cadets looked at each other and grinned. The officer felt uncomfortable, frowned and shooed him away from the patrol group. He believed that he should share the watermelon, and spoke of this with haste, whereupon the commander simply shouted at him to clear off. Realising that he was being driven away, he hugged the offering that had so angered these people and hastily asked just one question to find out what time it was. The duty officer's face froze in fear, yet also darkened ominously. Luckily for him, not far off some citizen at a loose end heard the question, looked at the clock hanging overhead in the waiting room and casually replied, telling him the time.

Knowing how long he had to wait for the train, he slowly paced along the platform. It was too cold to stand on the spot, and walking about with the watermelon was as oppressive as it was arduous. He did not dare throw it away, as he did not consider the money spent on it his own; it belonged to Abdulla Ibrahimovich. Feeling stupid and wretched, he suddenly thought of the hungry little girl who had once begged right in front of him. He could not remember what she had looked like, it seemed he had only felt her hunger – and at first slowly, then more boldly, he headed off in the opposite direction to that of his train. The rails covered everything as though they were waves, their steel crests gleaming in the moonlight, and it seemed as though they were even giving out a heavy murmur similar to the breathing of the sea. Underfoot the gravel was quietly gnashing its teeth. The cold of the steel river came alive with the coloured lights of the signals. The wind brought in turn the ethereal freshness of the cold and the shiveringly palpable drizzle, then the fumes from the sleepers with a hint of something burning – probably coal in the stoves of the trains racing past. He could clearly see the night when they had walked at this very hour, in this very direction, crossing the same silent expanse, and he realised with surprise that this had all happened before: only it had been without the heavy watermelon that he was carrying for the girl, thinking, for some reason, endlessly of her, not of the others who had also once been with him.

Dear readers,

We rely on subscriptions from people like you to tell these other stories – the types of stories most publishers consider too risky to take on.

Our subscribers don't just make the books physically happen. They also help us approach booksellers, because we can demonstrate that our books already have readers and fans. And they give us the security to publish in line with our values, which are collaborative, imaginative and 'shamelessly literary'.

All of our subscribers:

- receive a first-edition copy of each of the books they subscribe to
- are thanked by name at the end of these books
- are warmly invited to contribute to our plans and choice of future books

BECOME A SUBSCRIBER, OR GIVE A SUBSCRIPTION TO A FRIEND

Visit andotherstories.org/subscribe to become part of an alternative approach to publishing.

Subscriptions are:

£20 for two books per year

£35 for four books per year

£50 for six books per year

OTHER WAYS TO GET INVOLVED

If you'd like to know about upcoming events and reading groups (our foreign-language reading groups help us choose books to publish, for example) you can:

- join the mailing list at: andotherstories.org/join-us
- follow us on Twitter: @andothertweets
- join us on Facebook: facebook.com/AndOtherStoriesBooks
- follow our blog: Ampersand

Current & Upcoming Books

01

Juan Pablo Villalobos, *Down the Rabbit Hole*
translated from the Spanish by Rosalind Harvey

02

Clemens Meyer, *All the Lights*
translated from the German by Katy Derbyshire

03

Deborah Levy, *Swimming Home*

04

Iosi Havilio, *Open Door*
translated from the Spanish by Beth Fowler

05

Oleg Zaionchkovsky, *Happiness is Possible*
translated from the Russian by Andrew Bromfield

06

Carlos Gamerro, *The Islands*
translated from the Spanish by Ian Barnett

07

Christoph Simon, *Zbinden's Progress*
translated from the German by Donal McLaughlin

Oleg Pavlov is one of the most highly regarded Russian writers alive today. He has won the Russian Booker Prize (2002) and Solzhenitsyn Prize (2012) among many other awards. Born in Moscow in 1970, Pavlov spent his military service as a prison guard in Kazakhstan. Many of the incidents portrayed in his fiction were inspired by his experiences there; he recalls how he found himself reading about Karabas, the very camp he had worked at, in Aleksandr Solzhenitsyn's *The Gulag Archipelago*. Pavlov's writing is firmly in the tradition of the great Russian novelists Dostoyevsky and Solzhenitsyn.

Anna Gunin has translated *I am a Chechen!* by German Sadulaev and *The Sky Wept Fire* by Mikail Eldin. Her translations of Pavel Bazhov's folk tales appear in *Russian Magic Tales from Pushkin to Platonov* (Penguin Classics), shortlisted for the 2014 Rossica Prize. She has also translated poetry, plays and film scripts by Denis Osokin and Yuri Arabov.